Rienspel, Issue II:

The Village

Cover designed by Laura Faraci
To contact Ryan by email, send to: ryanpfreeman1@gmail.com
You can also follow Ryan via social media:
http://www.facebook.com/RyanPatrickFreeman
Twitter: @Ryanpfreeman
http://www.rienspel.tumblr.com/
Or just visit http://ryanpfreeman.com

Praise for *Rienspel*:

"*Rienspel* is a libation to the human soul. It is fantasy at its purest: a celebration of the myth, of the beauty of nature, of friends and family and forgotten goodness. The world and characters the author has created are simply unforgettable. Best of all, *Rienspel* is an unrivaled example of how fiction can indeed be true."
- R.E. Dean, Author of *Blood for Glory*

"Freeman's style combines a John-Grisham-suspense and a C.S. Lewis-high-fantasy flare, to keep his reader hooked. Page-after-page, I found myself wondering, 'what's going to happen next'. Readers will be asking for the sequel."
- Donna Lowe, Speaker and Author of *Radical Love...Forever Changed* and *Examine Your Heart*

"High adventure meets high-fantasy in *Rienspel*. In a world of tall trees and elves reminiscent of Tolkien or Terry Brooks, Freeman brings the inquisitive Rien to life in a Celtic inspired world. With a few twists along the way Rien's exciting adventure will carry you through to the very last page." - Brad R. Cook,
Author of *The Iron Horsemen Chronicles*

Chapter I
Choices

For space, all the boy could sense was the smell of Father Astor's freshly brewed tea and the old books, and the swirling dust motes in shafts of buttery yellow sunlight.

"Lllast night, a battle...women slaughtered...they were beautiful, innocent... and Centaurs... and death everywhere... and Murain... Murain and the others...they did it... and I did nothing!" he eked out. Rien stared, feeling empty and aching inside.

Father Astor gently embraced the boy, holding him close until most of the tears resided.

"Innocence lost," was all the old man spoke, sorrow lacing through every syllable. When Rien began to more or less compose himself he looked up into the old man's kindly face and sparkling eyes.

"Come. Let us step past so many prying ears into my study."

The Phoenix, unbidden, quietly fluttered along after them, fluttering amid the thick wooden beams high above.

Rien stumbled forward numbly, still rife with shock and horror. Past many rows of ageless scripts and dazzlingly illustrated vellum books, they strode until at last, they came to a round tower room. The aged door stood open, spilling bright morning light through the archway into the hall.

There was a chair inside the room. An old chair. Rien was surprised and delighted and momentarily forgot his pain. Out of the many, masterfully carved runes flowed too many colors to count. They flowed out of the study, mingling with the hues of beautiful stories upon the shelves, or the morning sunshine dancing joyfully on the floor.

"Ah, I see you like my chair. Please sit, it will help, I think. The cushions are soft and the sun is warming it, you see."

Silently, Rien sat. In moments, he was sinking softly into the loveliest chair he had ever known. He noticed his fear rolling out of him in dark waves, cascading harmlessly onto the smooth wooden floorboards.

"Would you like some tea?" Astor calmly indicated to the teapot on the wide, dark-grained desk next to the chair where Rien lounged, not speaking. "I always make too much for myself and try to share whenever I can," He said as he poured Rien a steaming cup and handed it to him. The old Rillian's eyes followed the Firebird's acute movements curiously.

"Have you never seen my chair before?" the old man inquired amiably, wrenching his gaze away from the fiery bird.

"No," breathed Rien. The boy tried to sip the piping hot tea but only succeeded in burning his tongue.

"Wait till it cools, there is always plenty more."

Carefully holding the cup, Rien began studying the many runes carved into the chair. "There are so many." The boy spoke, trying his hardest to not recall his black memories.

"Yes. Many letters. Many signs. Many stories, here in the wood," the russet cloaked man answered, gently stroking a curious series of seven large swirling symbols on the right arm of the chair.

Rien reached out his hand to trace the colorful swirls - which all glowed meticulously brighter under his gentle finger strokes.

"Ah, I see you have found your story," whispered Father Astor.

Beneath Rien, every hand-carved Rune glowed brilliantly.

"What do you mean? Can you see them too - the colors I mean?"

"Of course I can, you silly boy," chided Astor, who gave Rien a curious, perceptive glance from under his bushy eyebrows.

The Firebird, who had jumped out of Rien's open hands when he had reached for the tea, was now perched in his usual spot on the boy's right shoulder. Softly, he began to sing so close to Rien's ear. And slowly, courage seemed to course through the frightened boy's still shivering body. Peace flooded Rien's veins in a deluge of calm.

"Where did you get this fellow?" intoned Father Astor, his curiosity building perceptibly.

The Firebird fluttered down to the glowing, spiral carvings. All the colors suddenly diverted direction, swirling up around the bird's ever-burning flames in myriad hues.

"What is this?" voiced Astor, awed.

Slowly the multi-hued pantheon died down to embers. Rien scrutinized Father Astor carefully, unsure what to say.

The flaming bird gave him a knowing look and then began to nonchalantly preen himself.

"I… don't really know. I found him yesterday when I was out hunting… he keeps following me everywhere…"

"Rien... this... it is a Phoenix, Rien... They, or it, I should say, is incredibly rare. There is only ever one, you know."

"Hm?" the boy sighed, struggling to compose himself.

Father Astor sucked in a deep breath, as to launch into some long-winded explanation when outside the window; units of Rillian guards went marching smartly down the lane, sending a shiver of terror up the young boy's spine. Then all the memories of death and pain and innocence lost flooded back into Rien, bogging his mind in fear. Like a horrible nightmare trying to follow from dreams out into the waking world. Tears flooded Rien's brilliant blue-green eyes again.

Once the boy's blurry vision cleared he found himself in Father Astor's gentle embrace, slowly rocking him.

"It was horrible," Rien finally managed, through the pain.

And for what seemed like an age to Rien there was peaceful silence. His gaze drifted down to the morning sun filtering through the large, curved windows.

"Have some tea, it will help," Astor's deep voice suggested.

Rien raised the delicate cup to his lips and let the cozy liquid flow down into him, warming as it went. Hand in hand with the tea's warmth, relaxation washed over him.

"It tastes like... like pumpkin and cinnamon... like the autumn time when it rains..." Rien said, weakly smiling in spite of himself.

"Just so. It just came in this morning from an odd looking trader... from the North, I thought he was... called it 'Ch'I... or was it 'Kai'? Anyway, all I remember was how he kept his hood up and he told me if I ever wanted more, there was an inn halfway between here and Lymwall called The Green Siren I should look into... but enough of me. It seems the Stars have some twisted strand of choice before you, by the looks of it." He said, motioning to the brilliantly crackling Firebird next to Rien.

Impulsively, Rien felt an odd surge of childlike protectiveness over the glowing creature.

But Astor raised an old leathery hand to allay the boy's fear. "I mean the bird no harm, nor you. But I cannot ignore the runes on the wall, so to speak."

"I found him yesterday before I saw... I saw..." Rien swallowed and then continued, mustering his courage, "the battle" he finished.

And then a flash of recognition blazed in the irises of the old man. "Will you excuse me, Rien, I think I have just thought of a book which may help... just one moment, if you please," said Father Astor as he scurried out the door and into the hall.

While Rien patiently waited for what seemed like eons, he glanced around Father Astor's cluttered study. In front of him was a desk with half a dozen half-finished vellum manuscripts, stacked in messy, disorderly piles. A fireplace yawned to the boy's left, forgotten and sooty; just above the mantelpiece was a sleek saber with a darkened blade covered in scrawling runes.

Rien shivered involuntarily again, quickly raking his eyes away.

Two tall, arching windows directly across from Rien flooded the circular tower room with warm buttery light. Rien began to absentmindedly stroke the Firebird, his eyes catching painstaking detail which had been masterfully painted across the smooth masonry.

Immediately he recognized the story portrayed.

There, all around the room, the stones echoed the Fall of Rillium, the true home of all Rillians which they had been forced to forsake, fleeing for their lives across the sea in seven ships. There, Rien could see the King-to-be of Rillium dying before his gates on the eve of his coronation. There, the Russet Lord ran with many books weighing him down. The Blue and the Green Lords fought to give as many terrified people time to board the meager fleet. Just before the windows, Rien could make out the survivors meeting the Sirens on the floating Isle of Seriend. But he knew parts already... how the sirens had told secrets to the seven lords of Rillium... secrets bound in secret, known only to the Seven Lords. Then, after the windows, Rien saw the terrible storm. The walls seemed alive with the wrath of the sea... almost he thought he could hear the thundering waves... the doomed cries of the sailors struggling for their family's lives. Near the door, the waves carried the Grey Lord's ship and his entire house away, drowning them all in the watery depths. Lost forever was his part of the secret, for only he had known it. On the other side of the door, nearing the fireplace was the depiction of First Landing.

Six lords with six hues, armor stained in matching raiment, equipped as if for war strode forth upon six gallant steeds. They gazed intently at Rien from the wall...

"Like my dream..." murmured Rien, spellbound.

"What dream, my boy?" asked Father Astor quietly.

Rien gasped, surprised how the old man could move so stealthily. Out of his robes, the Waever brought forth a book so old it should be crumbling by every right. Father Astor quickly drew the long flowing curtains over the windows. Immediately the room was cast into darkness... only the light emanating from the Firebird remained. Curiosity filled Rien. He had never laid eyes on this book before. Where Astor had obtained it, he would probably never tell. Nevertheless, Rien's hands began slowly inching towards the tattered black book.

"I have written a rune over it, Rien. If you touch it, it will surely crumble into dust."

Rien quickly withdrew his hands but continued to stare eagerly at the curious symbols on the faded cover. Astor's hand tenderly traced eight multi-hued spiral shapes and a red flower with four petals of equal size.

Ever so softly, the Firebird cooed softly. From the look in its eyes, it seemed to be remembering something from ages and ages ago, but neither Rien nor Father Astor noticed.

"That's no Rillian book," whispered Rien.

"Do you know what this is, Rien?" Father Astor asked mysteriously, as he shut his door and swiftly locked it with a golden key he withdrew from a chain around his neck.

Rien shook his head, his eyes still locked on the ancient book.

"This is an Elven story. A history, really.... Or maybe it's just a legend, a myth."

"How did you ever get a Woodspirit story, Father Astor?" Rien asked incredulously, purposefully attempting to use the socially acceptable Rillian slang correctly.

"Elf, Rien, they much prefer to be called Elves. And no, Rien. I will not endanger you by revealing how I obtained this book. You know as well as me, important as I am, even I would be swiftly executed by the Emerald Queen for owning contraband like this."

Rien's face only fell slightly, but his eyes still remained intent and full of wonder.

"I can't read most of it, only understand gists here and there, you understand... but... it tells about what every elf either remembers or is told from childhood. In much the same manner as Old Rillium fell, they have lost a City too."

"Just like us?" – the question enraptured Rien.

"Yes," continued Father Astor, explaining, "It was a dreaming city full of light and music. Dancing and magic. Love and wonder... Only, I very much doubt there is anything left of it anymore to reclaim. Only memories remain now. Only the Necropolis remains..." at this, the old man grimaced and shook his white head slowly.

"But what does this have to do with my..." Rien searched for the right words and came up empty.

"*Your* Firebird? *Your* Phoenix?" Father Astor intoned as he flipped a few pages into the dusty copy. There, in between pages of queer, flowing letters were breathtakingly wondrous illuminated color plates. An older, more familiar terror washed over Rien, followed by intense sorrow as he looked and beheld the image. There, unmistakably, was Rien's Firebird, his Phoenix, rising from a once magnificent, now devastated city. Out of the ashes of a seven-paneled archway and myriad broken bodies rose the bird sitting calmly next to him. Rien could almost hear through the bird's raging inferno a breathtaking cry. But the bird was not alone. Plummeting down from the heavens were two titanic, blurry forms. One Rien recognized immediately as Azrael, Death; the other, some sickeningly beautiful god-like being with skeletal wings, crowned with razor-sharp horns and a long, barbed tail.

"No mortal knows his true name," whispered Astor.

Rien was shaking. Too many colors were bombarding his eyes to count... too many colors and then again, none at all.

This image was no recreation; it seemed as if whoever had painstakingly illustrated this horror's shade of history had actually been there. Blackened, tainted figures could be seen in the foreground writhing in agony.

Firmly, but gently, Father Astor delicately shut the tome. Life flooded Rien's pounding heart once more, and he took a deep breath, relishing the ability to feel the air in his lungs once more.

"It is The Fall, Rien, The Doom of this world and realm... and possibly for those who believe... it's salvation as well." Father Astor pronounced, shifting his glance from the quaking boy to his feathery companion.

Rien's eyes furtively slid over to the bird. Their eyes touched for a brief moment and the boy saw a bright shining hope he couldn't fathom exude from the Phoenix.

"I... know..." Rien wasn't sure of what he was saying; he only remembered what he saw in the Firebird's smoldering eyes. "It... He... showed me... I don't understand, Father Astor..."

"Stars are in motion I never dreamed existed," murmured the old man. After a long moment, he continued, "Rien, there is much I need to think about. You have no idea what this means, do you?"

But before Rien could answer, Astor swiftly tucked the book back into his billowing robes and began opening the windows and unlocking his door. "There is so much I... Rien, promise me you will look after this bird. Promise me." His usually kindly eyes bore dead seriousness.

"I promise, but what about last nigh...?" Rien began.

"I'll have to look into..." Father Astor began muttering as he paced to and fro.

"And what should I do about Vero…?"

"And I'll probably need to travel to Lymwa…" continued Astor, oblivious.

"And Murra…?"

"Delay the messeng…"

The old man began pacing and furiously scribbling notes on random pieces of parchment scattered about the circular room.

Rien stood up, not sure whether to stay or go. The Phoenix fluttered to his customary perch on the boy's shoulder.

"Rien," Astor took a deep breath, halting his relentless pacing, "Don't think I have forgotten about what you saw last night." The man took a breath and tried to gage the boy's reaction, then continued, "I know you saw things which young eyes should never have to see…"

Rien looked away and shuddered.

"My son, there is evil in the world - it's true. But it does not have to become us. Did you know this? It is how you choose to act because of it which can make all the difference. Courage to forgive, to understand, and to treat evil with justice and right action is what shall see you through - and light from the Stars where else." The old man tenderly smiled at the young Rillian.

"It's so hard, though. I don't know how I will be able to be the same around Veronjas."

"Ah yes, the Centauress. I thought I saw her in town earlier this morning… Rien, you have seen firsthand what hate-filled hands and sharp weapons can do, but there are stronger powers still."

"Runes…" whispered Rien, still not meeting Astor's steady gaze.

"Yes… and very much no. After all, runes are only symbols, expressions, for words which have meaning. Truth, if you will. And at Truth's core, there is love - and this is exactly what makes it powerful - Terrible even - in lives government by Truth. Terrible power to do Good. Which is exactly why all real Runes are bound in wisdom - otherwise they would simply remain funny looking symbols old men waste their lives over… or attempt to waste other's lives… all the same, it is my idea Truth is not the language we speak but the actions we live."

"Maybe…"

The old man's smile blazed.

"But what about Murain… how do I…"

"You are not the one to excuse his evil, but you can still treat him as your brother. Forgiveness is…"

"*Forgiveness?*"

"I will not force you to do anything… evil is not excused. But you need not hate in return like Cain once did, you know."

The boy shook his head, trying to understand. "Offerings to God were one thing… murder was something else…" he thought. Quickly, he wiped his eyes, downed his remaining chai and started for the door.

"You are a good person, Rien. And because of it, you are strong." Father Astor called, pouring a fresh cup of steaming, milky tea for himself. "Oh, and Rien..." the old Rillian paused, "I accept your petition for admittance into the Lycaenum. Be sure and pick up your initiate's cord on your way out."

"Thank you for the tea, it was really good." sheepishly admitted Rien "I..." he took a deep breath, for the first time fully realizing he had made his first life choice as a Rillian adult, "I will, Father."

"Know who you are, it's the key!" wafted the old man's low toned voice as Rien passed out of the main doors. "Now... to have a word or two with that gate guard..."

...

Rien sat on the front steps of the Lycaenum, enjoying the cool stones as the village sounds began to pick up all around him. The new yellow cord, comprised of three thick coils, felt strange but not altogether unwelcomed around his waist. A new sort of excitement swelled in his chest. Rien felt like he ought to walk around, silently announcing his long-delayed choice off for the whole village to see. A few blocks down, he could spy Murain's detachment marching down to the muster fields outside Nyrgen's walls.

"Off training and training... drilling and drilling..." mumbled Rien inside his mind.

And the boy wondered if he could ever forgive his older brother for murder. Glumly, Rien put his head in his hands and gazed up at the azure sky and at the myriad dandelion puffs floating on the summer winds.

"What you thinkin' about, Sucat?"

Rien jumped, startled out of his mulling. Standing above him, her head blocking out the fierce yellow sun was a girl. His heart jumped this time. "Kaylyn! I didn't notice you... I'm sorry."

She still waited, curious and expectantly.

"Oh, never mind, I don't really want to talk about it..." Rien half mumbled, his eyes still following the soldiers.

Kaylyn's eyes followed the uniformed boys too. "Something about Murain, isn't it?" She said softly.

"I guess..." Rien managed.

Kaylyn swiftly changed the subject, "have you talked to Veronjas yet? She's in town you know... got in early this morning." Her eyes flitted from the militia to the fiery bird on Rien's shoulders and then down to the new yellow cord draped casually around the boy's waist.

A well-concealed gasp escaped her lips.

"He's beautiful," she gasped, unable for more words; as the bird stretched its blazing wings lazily, basking in the sunlight. Finally recovering herself from the sight of this marvelous smoldering bird, her eyes caught another new thing, "Nice belt, by the way, too," she finished with a wry grin.

Rien smiled, looking at Kaylyn Stryaar for the first time. Her shoulder-length auburn hair fell wavy on her lithe shoulders, "well, lithe enough for a Rillian girl, at least," thought Rien, chuckling. She was slim but not sickly and armed with a dazzlingly white grin which stunned Rien every time he beheld it. His young heart was jittery whenever she was around... but he was never quite sure what to say either...

"Father Astor thinks it's a Phoenix... you know, a Firebird... I think it likes me or something, 'cause it won't seem to leave me alone..." explained Rien, his thoughts racing back to the flames and waters the other day at his thinking pond. He unconsciously rubbed his cord.

The Rillian girl sat down near Rien on the cool, worn stone steps.

The bird gave him a wry look and then took off, wheeling in the clear sky high above Rien and Kaylyn.

"Oh," said the girl, a little put out, "was it something I said?" Kaylyn paused for a moment and then asked, "Hey, you haven't seen old Voros around, have you? Bo's been acting kinda weird today. He's all stiff and silent... so has the rest of the militia, too."

Rien stiffened too, unsure of what to say. After hesitating a moment, the boy shook his head and then continued watching the mesmerizing darts and rises of the Firebird. It felt easier right now instead of trying to answer. The boy shook his head and cleared his mind with an effort.

Rien and Kaylyn smiled at each other, gazing up as the flaming bird swooped and dived.

"It's like it's free up there," spoke Rien.

Kaylyn sighed and pulled out her wood flute from a pocket, but kept her envious eyes on the Phoenix high above them and Rien's golden initiates bond. Kaylyn knew how much this choice must have meant for Rien. She knew it had been months for this stubborn village boy to make up his mind. And she also knew enough not to broach the subject – not now... not yet, anyway. Here and there, they could occasionally spot other enraptured villagers halting their work to gaze upwards at the Firebird soaring around the air, strong and free, high above.

"Where'd you get it?" asked Rien, admiring the flute's fine craftsmanship.

"I made it!" Kaylyn proudly exclaimed, jumping up. She started dancing along the top of the Lycaenum's waist-high wall, trilling snatches of tunes as she went.

Rien stood up too, intrigued, but mainly because his mind had drifted back to his conversation with Addios... about the Festival... about this dumb dance he really wanted to take Kaylyn to... "I didn't know you knew how to make 'em..."

"Well... I didn't use to... but, well, actually your brother taught me about a week ago... said he watched one of those funny looking goat men make one out of reeds once..."

Rien saw the green-tinged swirl of jealousy ooze out of him... "It's a good thing only me and my show off bird can see this..." Rien thought idly.

There in the late morning light, the golden rays danced off the girl his heartbeat for... matching the tune of her thin, reedy flute. He wished the moment could last forever. Gold colors eventually replaced the dingy greens exuding out of him, mingling with the pale, strawberry reds from Kaylyn...

And there she danced on the wall, carefree and lighthearted.

Rien sighed. "So this is what it's like to envy..." he thought, but his mood had changed, and the dark night terrors had momentarily lost their grip. There was only Kaylyn dancing to her own music on familiar streets - lovely and wild and free. Like the Firebird soaring above him.

They spent the rest of the day together, not caring or worrying. Rien found he was forgetting the pain more and more every minute he was around the girl. With every smile, he felt better. The two seemed to be naturally drawn to each other. It was common village knowledge about how Kaylyn's father had died when the girl was young. Some said an evil curse had slowly worked its poison through the kind man's veins; others claimed the Stars had something to do with it. Kaylyn had long since ceased listening to either... but Rien always wondered if she still missed him, and wished he were there for her, just as he desperately wished his own father were there for him too. At the very least, he was comforted by the thought that formal training for his new job wouldn't begin just quite yet.

On the inner battlement wall, they stood together at sunset, kindred spirits. Drawn into mutual friendship, Rien and Kaylyn's understanding of the same personal brand of pain was something which needed no words. Somewhere below them brooded Gateman S'ven, who was not in the least pleased at his towering son's nose being broken (they were having some difficulty resetting it). The boy, the girl, and the Firebird stared off into the darkening woodland as dusk's gentle melody replaced late afternoon. Soon the depths of mossy trunks were lost to the last soft rays of fading sunlight, melting into supple, silvery moonlight.

It wasn't until the moon had crested over the Gezronite mountains, spilling the quiet forests with early night radiance Kaylyn spoke what was on her mind.

"I'm really glad you're around, Rien..." she began, avoiding his gazing eyes lit by the Phoenix's steady orange blaze. Delicate, rosy pinks were flowing out of her - pinks edged in bread-colored browns. Rien wondered what this meant.

But all he could really see was a fair young girl dappled in flowing moonlight - soft and lovely. His heart yearned to say words his courage couldn't quite muster. So silence filled the gap instead, providing piercing conversation.

Finally, Rien screwed up his courage and asked, "Kaylyn, I was hoping with... with..." he gazed too fully into her curious chocolate eyes and tried to maintain his faltering momentum, "with Leunami coming up and all if you... well..." the boy took a deep breath, "if you wanted to go to the dance with me?"

There he stood as if on the subtle edge of a knife pressed firmly, tenuously against his furiously beating heart, waiting. The luminous shades around him were rapid, multi-hued wisps, making him appear as if he were steaming out his slightly pointed ears.

She flashed him her usual smile, but something in her eyes fell. Rien thought there was a strange mix of envy, as well. The knife slid into the young boy's heart causing him to sigh.

"I'm really sorry, Rien... but... well... your brother Murain already asked me a few days ago," she explained, shifting her feet on the creaky oaken planks.

Rien expected anger to rush up inside or even embarrassment... but instead, only sadness lingered in the very bottom of his crushed spirits.

One by one, the stars were coming out above their heads, brilliantly burning in whites, blues, and reds - countless and breathtaking. One could almost imagine hearing faint popping sounds as they unveiled their glowing light. Only crickets sounded in the deep sylvan quiet which surrounded them.

"How's your apprenticeship with Alormene coming?" Rien asked quietly, abruptly changing the subject.

The glowing embers of the Firebird floated lazily up like offerings to the majestic celestial heavens above them. Rien thought he could sense the girl's irritation towards him rise just a little.

"You know, at first I hated it… what with Alormene constantly comparing me to Addios… you know, before he had to join the guard and all…it's really nice how he gave me today off, though," Kaylyn said.

Rien could see Kaylyn's previous shades of awkward greenish tinged yellows fade into dark, luminous purples shot through with proud, flickering reds.

"She's actually proud of her work now…" Rien realized. He could remember when she had first been "asked" to fill Addios' vacancy at the woodcarver's shop.

"I'm just glad I don't have to march every day out in the fields," she smiled.

"Yeah, me too!"

She gave him a bemused look out of the corner of her golden irises.

"Yeah… the shop can get a little redundant sometimes… but what's it like in the Lycaenum?" she teased, over-emphasizing her last words, but Rien now distinctly realized she was jealous.

Rien let out a sigh, his mind bringing up endless droning hours of calligraphy, oral exercises, and dry history lessons he fully expected to have to sit through. "I don't think it'll be too bad… but sometimes I just… I don't know… I want to live life instead of merely hearing about others who lived theirs…"

"I wish I was allowed into the Lycaenum…" she said staring down and away moodily - the now year-old village scandal was almost forgotten (Rien thought he heard Kaylyn acidly mutter, "not magically gifted enough - pah!") "But I know what you mean… I think." The girl replied, her colors swirling and changing again.

"How?"

"Well, I feel kinda stuck sometimes… I touch pieces of scrap wood and I can tell just by brushing my fingers across the grains all the different ways I could use it. An arrow shaft here, a wagon spoke there… or rocking chairs or spinning wheels… but every once in a while," at this, the fire in her eyes sparked and raged, "I come across pieces meant for more… like… like… I don't know…" she ended, still grasping for the right words.

Rien was intent on Kaylyn's flowing fountain of colors while she spoke. As she tried to explain just exactly what she meant, Rien noticed all the dazzling ripples and patterns… and a sort of language to them… like they all meant something. He could tell just by watching intently who she was echoed questions and deep needs and wants. The boy snuck a furtive glance over at the cozy bird roosting between them.

Going out on a limb, Rien, while trying to gather the meaning of Kaylyn's colors, drew a breath and spoke, "I think you're one of those pieces…"

Her fountain sputtered, surging secret hope while coating splashes of doubt to guard against what Rien thought was some sort of angry red pain.

She huffed, "yeah, sure. Whatever Rien. It's easy for you… learning about all the great stories all day or slipping off into the woods… you're so free… and look at me… stuck. Always stuck and passed off."

Rien interpreted her colors again, clear and bright, but marred with sorrow. But the boy didn't need to ponder long to know what ached in his friend's soul.

"It's all about her father…" the boy thought.

"I'm not passing you off."

Kaylyn shot another complicated look at the boy. The Phoenix's light illuminated their arching eyebrows and cheekbones. "You just still want to go to the dance with me… and you're disappointed your brother asked me first…"

Rien peered over the battlements at the little glowing fireflies crazily dancing in the tall grass by the southern forest road.

"Yeah, you're right… but I still think you're more than driftwood, Kaylyn."

She was silent about this… her face became sour with irony, but her true colors simply gave her away.

"At least I'd be free then. Kinda like today, Sucat… Alormene let me off today… crazy old man thinks he's overworking me or something… ha!"

Rien grinned, "Yeah, let him keep thinking it… you only feel tired when you don't want to make the rest of us normal people feel bad we can't keep up."

The fire in her eyes returned, only burning softer now.

High above their heads, above the fireflies in the tall grass and the wind in the quiet trees, the moon soared ever higher.

Just the crickets and the crackling Firebird.

It was all so perfect. Rien half imagined he could hear the world around him singing softly – a lullaby.

"Thanks for talking, Rien… it means a lot to me." Kaylyn said as she got up and stretched.

The boy knew she was preparing to leave… and wishing beyond hope she wouldn't.

"I love talking with you Kaylyn, anytime."

She smiled. Her invisible swirling colors were far too complex for Rien to riddle out this time.

"Well, I gotta get home and sleep… I gotta be in the shop tomorrow to hear another of Alormene's tirades about Old Rillium."

She started walking towards the battlement's stone-hewn steps which would take her down to the quiet village streets.

"Hey, I really liked your music, you should really think about playing something for the festival…" called Rien.

"I'll think about it," she called dubiously, out of the supple night.

Rien smiled to himself and gazed at the stars for a little while longer. Once he started getting uncomfortable in how he was sitting Rien scooped up the dozing bird and slipped quietly away towards home. Once in his room, Rien carefully removed his new initiate's cord, then stripped off his outer clothes and crashed into his soft pallet on the sweet, familiar dirt floors he called home.

Chapter II
Strange Tales

Rien knew he was dreaming again. Yet this time there were not lords or ships or cities... only wondrous colors swirling all around him. Here and there shades glided which he never knew existed...

Rien was quite sure most of them didn't. They were too glorious for anything but the world of his dreams. He forgot about Murain and Veronjas there... He forgot about his grieving mother... Dreams gave him just the briefest of respite against the world he knew so well.

And eventually, the warm morning light came again once more, with welcoming arms for the slumbering boy and the Firebird beside him.

"Another day..." the boy mumbled, rubbing the sleep out of his blurry eyes.

And then Rien turned over and saw his older brother's empty pallet. Grief mixed with biting anger flared in his chest. Oblivious to the red and blue swirls filling his vision, the Phoenix called softly away up in the rafters in the tranquil morning light. Sullenly, Rien brushed his bed-head hair out of his eyes and got dressed. With pale flickers, the Firebird fluttered down to his usual spot on the Rillian's shoulder as the boy stepped into the main room.

It was empty.

"Maybe Mother was already off this morning, probably preparing some new addition for her festival market stand," Rien thought. The boy smiled with an annoyed sort of pleasure about how much he knew mother would be excited about his career choice.

Regardless, Rien felt worry suddenly flood him... until he spotted the kettle warming over the hearth flames. "What if she doesn't like my choice?" the thought arose, unbidden. It wasn't necessarily that he needed her permission or anything, but dealing with an annoyed mom was still one of his least favorite things in the whole world.

"Must be out for something," he muttered to the vacant room with bare, earthen walls.

Hurriedly munching breakfast, Rien's groggy mind slowly accelerated back up to normal speed. Once fully awake, he found himself mulling over what it would take to talk to Veronjas, let alone forgive Murain. Donning his tattered cloak to ward off the early morning chill, and making sure his new yellow initiate's bond was purposefully fixed about his waist, Rien left for the Lycaenum.

Officially studying under Father Astor would consume his life – already, Rien knew his unofficial classes with the scholar could typically fill up with everything from runes to understanding the ancient stories. Now that he was a formal initiate, Rien knew he would now be going beyond rote story learning… he had watched journeyman Rillian magi, or mages, come and go for years. Astor had usually just settled for quiet interviews before he awarded them his letter of recommendation before sending them off to the next town's Lycaenum or adventure… others who Father Astor had felt still needed proving he typically sent off questing nearby. The tasks, Rien noticed, were really little more than magical or alchemical grocery runs… but every now and again, a particularly inept or unlucky Journeyman would come back with burns or nasty frostbites, and minor poisonings… or curious minor curses, if they were really unfortunate.

Rien was still thinking about which subject Father Astor might be resuming today as he climbed the smooth steps up to the mighty double oaken doors of the Lycaenum. As he heaved the massive doors open and stepped across the rune-bound threshold, his mind wandered back to the forbidden Elven history his new master had shown him.

"How did he get it, I wonder…? It must be from Rillium… all the old treasures are, one way or another." At the end of the long cool hall paneled with cedar was Astor, leaning against one of the tall white pillars surveying the Master Story Atrium. As Rien approached closer, he could tell the old man was deep in thought, as usual. The deep brown wrinkles in his worn face were deeply lined, creased with ghosts from a faraway time, and his eyes still wandered distant lands across deep seas.

"Father Astor?" Rien asked, almost not wishing he had to interrupt the wise sage from his bittersweet nostalgia.

Astor's eyes hurtled back to reality in a flash, from long ago back to here and now. Rien wished he wouldn't have. The boy wished he could see into the man's past and witness exactly what Father Astor vividly saw in his mind's eye with clarity.

"Rien," the old man uttered quietly, "Have I ever told you The Rilliad?"

"The holy tale?" the boy asked, curiosity hinged his winged wonder.

"I realize you have heard some semblance of our story here and there… but have you ever heard the tale in full?"

"Well, if you put it that way, then no. I guess I haven't. I know I'm an initiate now, but why?"

The Phoenix on Rien's shoulder sang a flowing series of harmonious notes - a melody.

"Because of this bird on your shoulder, I suspect. But come to the Odeon of the Waevers…" he said, ushering Rien past row upon row of well-tended books to an illustrious archway scrawled in fiery, vine-like runes, "besides, you get the happy task of preparing the alternative rain room for the storytelling contest next week anyway… one can never be too prepared, you know," Astor finished cheerily, indicating a sloshing wash bucket and broom tucked near the entrance.

"Cleaning?" Rien sighed, his question more of an accepted statement than anything else. "You prepare and I will speak - unless you would rather start copying the entire Lay of Dardania into Dwarvish runes instead?"

Rien made a slight face, "the longest one on record right?"

"Well, besides the Rilliad, yes. This is why I will be telling it to you slowly, over the course of the week. I trust your apt, spritely young mind will commit it to indefatigable memory."

The boy sighed and picked up the mop bucket and broom, preparing himself through a quick series of diverse mental exercises. "I'll do my best."

"Well, if it's your best, I'm sure your recall will be immaculate next week."

Rien stopped cold. The Firebird squawked in indignation at the sudden movement, ruffling its flaming feathers in a shower of sparks.

"Me? At the barding contest?" Rien stammered, still shocked.

"Why yes, of course... you didn't think I would just let you sit here and gather dust every week like I do the books, do you? Besides, you're an initiate now, Rien. So try and take some pride in your work..." Father Astor replied with an amused chuckle.

"Right," the boy stated, shock numbing his system. He barely recognized his own emotion, which took on stark grey tones, cascading down onto the floor pooling about his booted feet.

In front of him stood the door.

Like a titan of old, it loomed. A flaming, dazzling woman stood, gazing back at Rien from the carved wood. Her eyes seemed to question and beckon all at once, and like an irresistible fate, drew him inside the room beyond. The familiar buzzing of Rune wards swarmed against his skin as Rien passed through into a mesmerizing chamber with a stained glass dome. The vastness of the Sanctum took his breath away. This was a room he had never been allowed in before - not until now. It was typically reserved for nobles and master story waevers only, not for rambunctious village youth like Rien. The stone and wood room had a colonnade bordering the edges, with a raised platform near the center. Across the floor were many, many runes and reliefs which were painted in dizzying arrays and patterns everywhere, all playing off the colorful light raining down from above through stained glass. The last detail Rien noticed was dust and cobwebs... the motes and webs floated along here and there, gently blown by some unseen air current.

Father Astor almost skipped to the center of the Odeon, and took a deep breath, collecting his thoughts. He cleared his throat and then noticed Rien still standing, gazing awestruck at the room and the lights.

"Rien. Don't forget your part of the deal..." the Sage gently reminded.

"Oh, right!" Rien sheepishly said, rather startled. Dutifully picking up the cleaning supplies, he began to clear the complex of cobwebs here and there. All the while, his ears were pricked and waiting, ready to remember whatever came out of the old man's lips. The Firebird fluttered up to some hidden rafter to roost meanwhile. Astor's old eyes searched, his mind settling on the right words which would begin The Rilliad, the tale of the loss of Rillium and the destruction of his old home across the seas...

...

Rien's mother had been ecstatic when he returned home for the midday meal that day. Later in the evening, the whole family had gathered around their small table for a celebration. His mother had decorated their home with what little decorations she had tucked away or could borrow from others around the village. Rien, while pleased for all the positive attention for a change, noticed Murain seemed noticeably put out. They didn't seem to speak much after the night Rien had been locked out...

his older brother seemed distant now... and far more subdued than normal. After his mother began asking awkward questions about how Voros was becoming noticeably absent around town, Rien desperately found a way to change the subject.

After the festivities, Rien and Kadierie slipped out for a walk (and a flap) in the early summer nights' air where they ran into Kaylyn. The boy couldn't help but bring up how different Murain had been acting around him. The words and the questions just seemed to tumble one after another out of his heart. She tried reassuring him it must be how Murain probably just wished Rien had chosen to join the Militia with him... maybe his older brother was a bit jealous...

"Jealous? Of me?" Rien had replied disbelievingly.

"Sure, Rien," she had explained, as if trying to explain simple sums to Gateman S'ven, "The Lycaenum is prestigious, you know..." she told him exasperatedly, envy pouring out of her like a waterfall now, "and I also know Murain feels like the Militia is more... I dunno... Rillian... of the two choices - plus your father served in it, too."

While he still wasn't sure what exactly it was he wanted to do about Murain, Rien now was convinced of one thing: whatever his older brother was doing or becoming - he wanted absolutely no part of it. With strength from his new found aversion and irritation, Rien found himself practicing harder than ever... And every day the old Father assured him he was progressing. As the boy spoke, he began to move past the story into the rhythm of the words themselves. He could feel their ebb and flow, like some mighty tidal flow which went coursing through sentences and expressions. Rien began to understand where the natural pauses should be, where the paragraphs indented and where silence lingered. Stories and even regular speaking became a sort of chant - an incantation with a melody all its own.

Story was more than history, it was magic itself. Rien loved it whenever he could feel his hair rise with excitement or anticipation for some particularly compelling moment. Each time he continued his work with Father Astor over the Rilliad, he found himself wishing the King hadn't had to sacrifice himself before his city gates so the rest could escape on their ships out to sea. Each time he heard the Siren's call, he too yearned to draw just a little nearer, oblivious of all mortal danger. Each time the prophecy was given, Rien hungered to know just what, exactly, it meant. When the great sea storm came, like some wrathful god of old, bearing away the Grey Lord and all his people, the boy found himself wishing he could still somehow save them. Later, after the bedraggled Lords had landed on the Dardania shores, Rien recalled his dream some nights before and wondered. So many people... so much hardship-steeled wills and long-enduring hope was wound up in The Rilliad. Within its' cycles, his people's drive, and thirst for grand enterprise, which had hitherto been unknown to Rien, now proudly unveiled itself, clear as day. Even now the boy could feel his own place within the proud House of Rillium's enduring legacy, deep down within himself. It was a calling, a destiny, a summons to and from the beyond.

With a glance, he saw the sparkle of recognition glimmering in the irises of Father Astor. The old mage had felt it, too.

Outside, the little village of Nyrgen began to pick itself up in preparation for the swiftly arriving Festival of Leunami. Each day the picturesque town altered. When Rien would clamber, mind-weary, from the Lycaenum, the familiar scene of home shifted. First, the trash was all dutifully picked up. Then the signs were painted and the fronts all swept. Then the guards' newly polished armor glinted in the setting sun. The atmosphere picked up, taking on a jovial feel. People bustled jauntily along. Unspoken excitement tinged the air like a summer's storm.

As Rien and the Phoenix would hurry home, he reflected on how good it was that most Rillians were already accustomed to magical appearances. Nearly everyone had taken one curious look at the fiery bird often perched on Rien's shoulder, then glanced down at his golden initiate's cord and chalked the whole matter up to Lycaenum business. What did it matter to them so long as young

Rillian girls and boys kept in line with custom? The day before the day of the festival, Rien strode out, exhausted, but satisfied from his final Lycaenum secession. The town before him glittered like newly fallen dew. Here and there strung along fine, taught threads flickering golden stars twinkled, and in every lighted window glittered and shone even more Leunami stars. Illuminated with little candles and painted whimsical colors often used to represent the traditional seven loyal Rillian houses. The Stars of Leunami rose up from the humble earth decorating the village like a flickering field ripe for harvest.

Happy and tired, Rien trudged home. His body guiding him on, leading more off of instinct than conscience memory, he labored onwards in hope of comfort and dinner. He took a turn and crossed the main road when suddenly the gates at the far end burst open. Rien turned to watch, quietly slipping into the growing shadow of a building.

"OY, I am Chief Porter of Nyrgen of the Emerald Queen and Green Lord and I..!" screamed an old familiar voice.

In charged a group of strange Rillians on massive horses bearing strange flowered tokens. It took Rien a moment to realize many of them were from different Rillian houses! He had only occasionally seen Blue messengers... but this... Wow! This was completely new to him. There were all sorts of different Rillians: grim black riders; were noble Greens; fierce, wild-looking Reds; a few stoic Browns all thundering down the lane - the indignant cries of Gateman S'ven still rang out through the air - purposefully and idly ignored.

"Who are they?" Rien wondered out loud.

"Crusaders," an unbidden answer came.

Rien jumped. "Kaylyn," he breathed.

"Never thought I'd see the day when I could sneak up on you, Sucat."

"Yeah, well..." he mumbled, still in awe of the crusaders, as they made their way over to their village's only inn, The Gull's Cry, talking boisterously amongst one another. After the strangers dismounted and ventured inside, Rien turned to Kaylyn and resumed their conversation, "So how do you know they're crusaders? What exactly are crusaders, anyway?"

The girl rolled her eyes, "I thought you'd be the first to know – you're so weird with how you're always trying to chat with travelers when they turn up here... no, I overheard the smith talking about it - guess he's been commissioned to make weapons for some knight and his men-at-arms or whatever. Something about Woodspirits, actually... I guess."

"Woodspirits?"

"You know, Elves or whatever...Oh yeah, apparently they have this tree or something way down south," she pointed vaguely away to her left.

"Tree?" Rien's muddled mind conjured up Rilliad-esque visions.

"Yeah - Rien. A Tree. You know, big wooden things with leaves... we live in the middle of a ton of them called a forest. By Poseidon, I don't know how Father Astor picked you out of all of us for all the story stuff, anyway..." She looked down and away, off towards where a group of militia soldiers, Murain among them, were dispersing off home.

Rien noticed. "Still, uh..." he could feel his mouth go dry, "still going to the dance with Murain, huh?"

She gave him a mysterious look, "Oh, yeah, I guess."

Now it was Rien's turn to look down and away.

Just then Kadierie swooped down, cheerfully landing on Rien's shoulder and nipped his ear affectionately. Barely registering the deluge of swirling colors re-swarming his vision, he bade Kaylyn good night and resumed trudging slowly off home, admiring the hanging stars every now and then with a sigh.

...

Rien saw a slight figure slip in through the gates just before they shut fast for the night once more. Curiosity began to creep up in his chest again like some playful kitten bound and determined to mischief-make still. The decidedly odd figure began uncertainly making his way toward Rien, who stood in a single patch of warm wavering candlelight from the dancing golden stars strung above his head. The sun had just finished setting - its last long dull red rays leaking into the soft warm shadows cast by the festival decorations. In the gentle gloom, Rien attempted to discern the figure approaching. He was hooded, held a long polished staff and carried a tattered pack. The visage would have been normal enough, except he was so short... only maybe five or six feet tall – at best only coming up to Rien's chest.

The boy gasped.

"Harken, stranger! I uh... beseech thee... is this truly the realm of the Lord of Green... the Green Wood? I... um..." he halted for a moment to pull out a ponderous tome and began frantically leafing through, apparently searching for something. Soon the figure began muttering to himself...

"Greeting... Greetings... Grants.... Granite... Grab... Gravity... Greens... Giants..."

Rien took a few strides and approached the newcomer, unsure whether to be wary of the strange staff, which seemed to faintly glow and hum of its own accord. Ought Rien laugh at the odd, comical figure...? Even upon coming closer, it was hard to say... The boy could easily make out the old-fashioned style of clothes the stRanger bore, more to the taste of Father Astor maybe - or something out of the pictures he had seen of Old Rillium, even. Curiosity peaked within Rien. His eyes settled on the book open in the young man's hands. The words were funny... they were angular - like Dwarf runes, but different... more refined, perhaps.

The young man glanced up and up at Rien and blinked. "Gosh, you're tall!" He squeaked before he could help himself.

Rien couldn't help but laugh. "I would say you're short, but I can see you're no Rillian! Hey, where are you from, stranger?"

"Well, I'm from East Damros originally, but more recently from Shione."

"You came all the way from Shione!? Whoa! What's the Blue Lord's capital like, anyway?"

"Well, it's ah... it's ... hey, wait for a second, you understand me! How?"

Rien looked perplexed. "Uh... words? ... I guess?"

"Words, huh... words... words... words!" Each time as he spoke, there came a new inflection. "Brilliant! Just brilliant! Owaya of East Damros!" He cordially extended his little hand and shook Rien's massive, enveloping grasp, smiling, "But most people back at the college just called me Soph... and you are...?"

"Rien Sucat of the Green Wood, I suppose," the Rillian replied, laughing, "Pleased to meet you, Owaya... I mean Soph... so, um... are you here for the Festival, then?"

Soph dropped his book in excitement. "Festival?! What glorious design is this! What an amazing chance to learn first-hand all there is about Giant's culture! Tell me, what are your primary agricultural resources and the state of your pottery manufacturing during this particular epoch??"

Rien was bewildered. "Uhh... tell you what... how about you come home with me... mother usually sets an extra place anyways..."

"Splendid! I would be honored Rain Sucat of the Green Wood!"

The pair began to head towards Rien's home, as Soph looked wildly about chattering ceaselessly. Rien was enthralled - Soph's energy was an infectious sort.

"It's just Rien," the Rillian attempted to correct the inquisitive traveler.

"Giants often go by first names in traditional social settings..." he muttered as he furiously scribbled in his book, "this IS a traditional social setting, right??" Soph asked, whipping his head up.

"Um...Sure."

"Right! Right then!" He paused to gaze up at the dangling stars lit by little flickering candle stubs inside mounted everywhere. "And these, my good giant... are these some sort of street illumination? Some marvelously ingenious design? Dwarven make, perhaps?"

"What, the stars? No, they're just decorations for tomorrow's Festival of Leunami." Rien shut his eyes. All the wonderful, delicious memories of all the best Festival moments came flooding back... "It's great! All the work is put off for a day and there's feasting and music and dancing and lights and colors and then..." he lowered his voice to a mock-conspiratorial level, "The Stories."

"Stories?" whispered Soph, matching his tone - drinking in Rien's every word.

"Stories." Rien confirmed, glancing around for would-be eavesdroppers, "This is the first year I'm entering the competition. I've been practicing for weeks now." He quickly studied the new comer's face and decided he could be trusted with this top secret, confidential information, "I'm going to tell The Rilliad - complete and unabridged."

"The Rilliad. The Rilliad! ...What's a Rilliad?"

True dark enveloped them now like some soft blanket, ushering in a chorus of unassuming crickets as they walked on. Rien purposefully slowed so the much shorter-legged Soph could keep pace. All around them the hanging stars were glowing brighter as the darkness deepened and the light became their only source to see the humble village roads as they passed them by.

"Oh, well, um, the Rilliad is a lot of things actually. It's an epic, really. It's about my people, the Rillians, and how we came to settle here; on the continent we call Dardania. For some of the older Rillians, it's real history though, because they actually came off the ships or are the original settler's children. The six surviving Rillian Lords were actually there!"

"Wait! Wait, wait, wait, wait!!" puffed Soph.

Rien halted and turned. He just now realized Soph had been writing while they were walking. Apparently, he was trying to get as much word by word as he could. The Rillian laughed in spite of himself.

"I'm sorry, Soph. If I had known you were trying to write all of this down I would have gone slower. "When I was learning the Rilliad from Father Astor, – he's Nyrgen's resident Master Story Waever – he was always going too fast for me too." Rien caught more quizzical looks from Soph and then took another breath and continued explaining, "Oh, wow. I forget you really don't know anything! Well, let me see here… Story Waevers are people who in my culture are more like professional storytellers."

Soph began dabbing bullet-point outlines all over a fresh page now.

"They remember our people's history: all the great deeds and lasting moments of times long ago. Each tale is carried on from Waever to Waever, and recorded in Lycaenums. Without them, we'd really be in the dark. Master Story Waevers are in charge of preserving, remembering and collecting as many stories as possible."

Soph nodded as Rien briefly paused to catch his excited breath.

"Waevers, in turn, teach the tales to new apprentices, who in turn learn from each other, and together everyone tries to apply what they learn for helping others. It's simple, I think…"

Soph frowned, concentrating on finishing his line with a flourish.

"Father Astor is the oldest Rillian I know, come to think of it… I never thought about it, but I guess it means he was probably there when the Rilliad happened…!"

Near a particularly bright gathering of glittering, hanging stars Rien stole a glance at the furious letters Soph was frantically scribbling. "Hey, what are those!?" the Rillian asked curiously.

"Words." barked Soph, still writing like mad.

Rien rolled his eyes, but attempted to steel himself against impatience, "Yes, I know they're words – I'm Father Astor's apprentice now" said the Rillian, indicating towards his initiate's cord, "But they're not at all like the words I know how to write. What is it, anyway?"

Soph wrote on doggedly, "Show me what your words look like," he said, not looking up, "do you have an alphabet or something… could you write it down for me here, please?" He waved his open book over and up to Rien.

"Um, well, sure I can… um…" Rien said as he delicately took the book and the tiny writing utensil and began scratching carefully, "There. There it all is – all forty-two of them used…" his eyes carefully skimmed the last paragraph Soph had written. The letters curved and dived vastly different from the Rillian characters… he stared for a moment more, tenderly stroking and tracing the words… then stared a bit more. Rien took in a quick gasp. They were beginning to make sense to him somehow.

Has there ever been a moment where something which for ages had been meaningless noise and confusion suddenly coalesced, as if by magic, into meaning and purpose right before the very eyes? It was something a bit similar for Rien, too.

The Phoenix fluttered down onto Rien's shoulder - and the page lit up with its brilliant colorful light of the fiery bird. Then Rien could see clearly. He could read Soph's writing. Every word. Every inch. Rien flipped back to the beginning and began reading, slack-jawed in amazement. "Hey, your alphabet only uses twenty-six letters…" Rien murmured, stopping and looking back down at Soph.

"Father Astor's apprentice, did you say?" was all Soph was able to verbalize in astonishment.

"Yeah, why? … How long did it take you to read?"

"About a year – in my own language," was all the stRanger could squeak, yet again.

Remembering what he had read from the beginning of Soph's travel journal, Rien asked, "Is it true you come all the way from the Isles of the Sea Kings?! Incredible! Why, it's almost to Old Rillium, itself, if I remember rightly! What are you doing way out here in the middle of the Great Woods?"

Soph, still eyeing Rien with newfound respect, replied, "I think it would be best if we shared all this over a dinner." The stranger's stomach rumbled, as if on cue. "I'll be more than happy to tell you everything."

The pair rambled off for home in the candlelit evening, the long shadows and golden haloed lights of the decorative stars rippling by as they passed, chatting animatedly.

The front door squeaked as the pair entered Rien's cozy home. Inside, the dinner table, laden with hearty fare, glowed with long, careful years of scrubbing. Rien's mother glanced up from setting what appeared to be the final plate down and smiled warmly at her youngest boy and the unexpected guest. The Firebird took off to perch watchfully on the gable, assuming its nighttime post.

"Hello, I'm Kassandre Sucat, you are welcome in my house tonight," she greeted the new guest, nervously eyeing the single, extra chair which usually always remained ceremonially empty, and sighed just a little. Then, with a sudden start, her eyes widened at the flickering bird nestled snuggly in her wooden house. "WHAT IS THAT!! Rien - get it out! Murain, quick - fetch the buckets and run to the well!!"

Rien laughed. He had been wondering how long it would take for mother to finally notice the Firebird. Getting the better of his mirth, he attempted to calm his mother, "It's alright, its ok! I found him in the forest a little while ago – it doesn't actually light anything on fire... so far... This is Kadierie, everyone."

Kadierie nimbly dodged a particularly wild broom-swing from Kassandre and twitter a jaunty little song back down at her, settling once more on a higher rafter just ever so slightly out of the woman's reach.

Murain eyed the creature dubiously, "so long as it doesn't incinerate us, I don't care what it is," he grumbled. Then, with a big stretch, the tired Militia soldier decided to just start ignoring the thing. Murain's little brother's oddments nettled him all the more, though. From the far end of the table, Murain just kept lounging, attempting very hard not to immediately bolt down his dinner. Taking a breath and controlling himself, he called, "Hey Rien - it's about time! We were starving!" He glanced over to the stranger and darkened his voice a bit. He did not hold with Rien's fondness of foreigners. "And pray tell, what is your name, little stranger?"

Soph, profoundly oblivious to Murain's moody undercurrent, replied cheerfully, "I'm Owaya of the Isles of East Damros..." His introduction was met with blank stares - Rien was really the only one in the family with a head for maps, "...of the Isles of the Sea Kings. But most people just call me Soph," he finished, helpfully.

Murain momentarily forgot his prejudice and exclaimed, "He's almost from Old Rillium itself!"

Kassandre's eyes bulged incredulously too. "Here, take a seat. Tell us more of your travels, Soph."

Rien caught his Mother biting her lip, their eyes locking in understanding. "It'll be alright, mother, he would want it this way, helping guests out of the night and all..."

Kassandre finally assented with a stiff nod.

Soph reluctantly took his seat, "I'm sorry if I'm not so familiar with traditional Rillian customs... have I infringed upon something?"

The silence in the room thickened. Murain glared. Kassandre busied herself with clattering forks and knives. Only Rien tore his eyes off the floor to explain, "Our father was a message rider for the Green Lord. His circuit would ride between Lymwall, the capital of the Green Realm we are citizens of, the one in which you are now in, to Shione in the blue realm. A long time ago he was returning from Shione with an important message when he... got lost. We don't know what happened to him... since then...You're sitting in his chair."

"Oh," was all Soph could manage, feeling increasingly uncomfortable.

Kassandre finally sat up, apparently satisfied with the utensils, "My son is right. It is the way Ossolon would have wanted it. Imagine the height of discourtesy if we couldn't even give a tired traveler a place at our own family table. Please, sit, and dine with us tonight. Tell us your story."

Soph stopped fidgeting for a moment, and turned to her, "My lady, it would be my honor."

And Rien could feel he really meant it.

"Well, let's not wait a moment longer. Murain, would you please offer the prayers tonight before our guest begins?"

Rien watched as his older brother dutifully scrapped the choicest cuts from the serving dish, along with a splash from the table wine into their cheery hearth, and gave a silent prayer Rien knew was directed towards Poseidon, whom all Rillians claim as their Father; and to Hestia, the patron of hearth and home. He uttered another prayer for their long-lost father. The fire crackled and sizzled as the prayer was engulfed by the flames. Rien still avoided Murain's eyes, but he remembered how purposefully prideful his older brother was over religious duty. Somehow, his older brother's convictions unsettled him. Out of the corner of his eye, Rien could see Soph hastily jotting notes in his tattered journal and smiled.

Murain resumed his seat. Kassandre began to serve them each in turn, beginning with Soph first, then Murain, then Rien and lastly herself, and then settled back into place.

"So, let's hear this story! Rien exclaimed.

Soph took a breath, steadied himself with a draught of table wine, and began, "Well, if you don't mind, I think I'll save the full tale for the Festival, Rien here has just informed me of... let me see..." he began rummaging around in a traveling satchel for his well-worn journal, "ah, LAY-UN-NEMI."

Murain rolled his eyes.

"But I was born on an island far off into the West, called Owaya. Soph is just a nickname, of course. My real name is Owaya... my people use where they are from as last names, typically. In a floating of scattered isles, it's the best way to keep track of where everyone's from. Anyways, when I came of age, I sailed to the Isle of the Wise, the largest of the islands ruled by our Empress of the Western Seas and the four kings."

"How many islands are there?" asked Rien, who was having some trouble wrapping his mind around the breadth and scope of this far-distant land.

Soph grinned, "Ah, well... that's a matter of some debate... some islands come and go with the tides... others are just rising up from the depths of the deep as we speak. Some..." he paused here for dramatic effect, "SOME can only be found by certain people on certain days and one is only visible every other Thursday."

All this puzzled Rien immensely.

After a moment's pause, Soph continued, "Anyways, we sailed to the Isle of the Wise... and to help pay for my passage, I used some of my skills to help speed the voyage and entertain the crew with tales from my island which every farmhand knows... regardless, the other sailors must have liked hearing them, because every night I remember they would roar for me to repeat some part or tell 'ANOTHER!'... As payment, one of the old merchants gave me this..." Soph held up an ancient, shining coin with the clear image of a circle emblazoned in seven pieces. One of the colors of the pieces matched the reverse side of the coin, where the inscription of a beautiful city could be seen arching and soaring proudly between two mighty rivers.

The Phoenix tilted its feathered head and cawed.

Rien felt like he ought to know the image... but the edging feeling slowly slipped away back into oblivion as Soph re-pocketed his treasure.

Soph shot Rien an odd, intentional glance, and then continued, "I earned my name and my staff there, as my people say. Oh, how I loved combing their libraries... the special rooms where they kept the strange books the whalers would trade for canvas or dried fish... somewhere away off in the Eastern Mainland, they said they found them... it's part of the reason why I eventually traveled here and can sit in your hospitable home today, actually. I'm story hunting. Trying to trace myths and legends and dictionaries back to their sources..."

"How are the books strange, exactly?" asked Kassandre.

Soph's eyes twinkled, "Ah, well... hem... that's the twist, isn't it... they're all written in the strange languages... the same strange language, to be exact. They claim they're published in cities which, as far as we know – and we know quite a bit – don't exist. They use ways of dating time which no one we've ever come across uses as if their very sun and moon were different. Some of them even are written as if they assume the same historical events and figures, too... It is truly a strange matter... Anyways, I intend to track down just exactly where these Whalers obtain them. And so here I stand before you now."

"You're here for a bunch of moldering old books?" Murain asked in disbelief. "What about Old Rillium... do you know anything about there?"

Soph paused, a troubled expression flashed across his face before he finally responded, "Well yes... and no... we do not sail that way anymore. The ships which did never came back. It began several generations of my people ago... say... a hundred years or so..." He shifted uncomfortably.

"Hm..." Murain grumbled.

"Rien, perhaps I could enter the contest, too? If it's not too late?" Soph asked.

"Sure, just go talk to Father Astor. He's the head of the Lycaenum here in town... the one who's been training me for tomorrow. Just go talk to him in the morning... the contest doesn't really start until sunset, after the lighting of the twin fires," the boy quietly answered.

The fire and the candles had begun their hypnotic dance as the four ate the evening meal together. Long shadows began dancing their quick dance between the angles in the room. Above their heads, across a sturdy wooden beam, a golden star danced ever so slightly as night drew on.

Just before everyone had concluded dinner, it was Murain who broke the silence, "How did you get here, then? Why are you even in Nyrgen, stranger?"

For a moment, the quiet re-enveloped the room, and then Soph replied thoughtfully, "By boat of course, and then my own two sturdy feet from there on. I've been on a literary trail, one might say..."

Soph reclined, relaxing his tired calf muscles. The fire and the warm familial setting cast his mind far away over distant seas to his own home and family... After noticing the family's expectant expressions, he continued musing... "Once I did reach my college... You can, of course, hear my full tale in its entirety tomorrow, but I think I'm just coming to now realize how much college – learning - is not a place. It's a place of mind - an attitude. The whole world is like some grand book or library. Full of daring and danger... and learning and hardship... and everything else in between..." he yawned, sleep gently itched his drooping eyes now.

"Well, that must have been some boat, then!" exclaimed Kassandre.

Soph smiled, "to answer your question more fully, I got here on a boat I learned to construct from other books at my college. My boat, the Merry-Weather, was made partly of metal similar to my coin and initially self-propelled. But this is a story for another day..."

"What are the Whalers like, and where do you think your books really come from?" asked Rien.

"Hm? What's that? Oh, the Whalers... well, for years now, Rien," he turned now to face Rien directly, "My people have traded with whalers of the Northern Ocean Vaste, who in turn trade with others who live far in the north of here. And they tell of another desert far away in the east, full of dunes and curious, dangerous little grey flowers. These grey flowers grow without water up from the reddish dunes which stretch as far as the eye can see. However," he intoned carefully, "They do not grow up one narrow canyon which snakes its way from the northern people's land deep into the desert, to a sort of dry lake bed. It is said when the moon is high and the north wind howls, the bed fills with water. In a flash, the sandy bed transforms from dry as a bone to brimming in seconds. No living soul knows from whence the water comes, but they say it is warm salt water as from a great southern gulf. When the water rushes away like summer lightning down away to the great ice bays of the north, it leaves behind great rusty metal... things. The people there call it the Circle of Redd." He finished ominously.

"Things?"

"Things... they are reportedly hard to describe. But some are like my little boat, except much, much larger. Others are made from the same metal, except they are broad and squat and flat, with little glass bumps full of more metal sticks. The people have made a habit of carefully dismantling and transporting what they can back to their cities to make whatever use of it they can... but every now and again..." Soph looked around suspiciously, and lowered his voice even more, barely more than the hearth crackles behind him, "they find books."

"Books?" Kassandre Sucat asked, not lowering her own voice.

"SHHHHH!! Keep your voice down, if you please, Ma'am,... these books say all sorts of things... and the ones my college can glean off the whalers... they are REAL."

"Real?" snorted Murain, "of course they're REAL. You didn't eat any more Pushkin berries in the Green Wood, did you?" apparently amused at his own witty insult.

"I certainly hope not, my good sir! But Rien, they are histories and non-fiction and biographies and calendars and lists and manuals and magazines and children's tales!"

Everyone paused, unsure as to the sanity of their guest now.

"Rien, they aren't from this world. They can't be. Some at my college would call it blasphemy... but I have read the texts, as many as I could gain access to, and they all correlate. But none of it is from here, not even close. They're all from different publication dates and publishers... made up lands which don't even come close to a place here in our world... I've checked."

"Soph, what does this mean?" asked Rien, enthralled.

"I don't know, Rien, I just don't know. But I intend to find out... I told those at the college we ought to send an official envoy over to investigate this canyon ourselves... but they wouldn't hear of it. They forbade me to go... so I... ah... applied some of my knowledge in ship-building and... well, you get the idea. Besides, my people's understanding of the mainland here where you live is antiquated at best."

Murain still appeared nonplussed as his mother began clearing the table. Something about the newcomer both fantastically intrigued him and sickened him all at once... "Nonsense... all utter nonsense... and Rien's just eating this rubbish up." His glare followed the stranger to bed, as Soph lay down near the dying fire on a tattered bedroll sometime later.

Murain's final tired thought before closing his heavy eyes echoed in his mumbling mind, "...Ridiculous..."

...

There is a moment within every child where the moments leading up to a great event, holiday or summer break slows with tremulous excitement. Time appears to slow and every moment is consumed with the swiftly arriving future promise of fun, excitement, and wonderment. Rien lay awake for a long while, listening to the creaks in the house, filled with a thoughtless thought, an expression verging on a waking dream. He was excited, and nervous about the coming festival. Almost, Rien felt as he lay underneath the warm covers, he could forget the skirmish in the woods. And managed, just managed before finally dropping off, to forget his older brother, snoring near at hand, had ever been a part of it at all.

Chapter III
At the Festival of Leumani

T he morning sunshine playfully filtered into the room, warming the rich amber tones of the support beams arching overhead. With a lurch, Murain woke up. Stumbling around, in his usual morning stupor, the first thing he noticed besides the weather was how his brother was already gone.

"Out and ready for the Festival," he muttered as he finished dressing.

"More like out and skipping off on chores," teased the sunny, familiar voice of his mother from the next room over. "He left early with the stranger, off to the Lycaenum, I think."

"Haha," Murain called as he straightened some of his gear, already mentally categorizing which items he would need for his uniform for the parade later this afternoon. "Have you seen my dress uniform and my boots anywhere?" he asked as he entered the main room and sat down heavily at the table.

Out of well-practiced familiarity, his mother brought over a steaming pot of dark, rich coffee for her son. He always was a slow starter, despite the usual hours he kept serving for the town militia. The pungent aroma of the black liquid filled the room like temple incense offered to Poseidon himself. After serving up some porridge for two, along with some freshly sliced apples she carefully brought the two plates and bowls over and sat down across from her first born. Kassandre attempted to avoid the empty chairs on either side of them, but couldn't after a particularly loud pop crackled out from the morning fire.

Murain noticed. But what was he supposed to say? Dad was gone. Had been for years. He was probably dead. Murain felt certain. Even though sometimes when he was alone, the nagging suspicion still lingered somehow, against time and chance and circumstance. Perhaps he was wrong. Suppressing the whole internal mess was a practiced art by now. One which he executed without much extra thought as he began eating, after the customary offering. Glancing up, he caught his mother's anxious expression. Sometimes she would get this way. As if she was some sort of seer of old, able to hear the wind and read the waves, and speak the future. Dare he ask? After quickly debating the question with some ruthless logic, he softened. Staring up into the rafters high above, he saw the glinting stars.

Sigh.

He opened his mouth to speak, after readying himself with a sip of delicious coffee. But Kassandre Sucat beat him to it.

"I worry about you, Murain."

"Here we go…" he mentally groaned.

"My son, I…" she caught herself unconsciously beginning to shift her gaze towards the empty chairs and continued, "You seem tired. Have you been getting enough sleep? You were gone late several nights ago. I don't like it when that captain fellow keeps you out so long…"

"Mom," he reached his long arms across the smooth table and took her hands tenderly, something about the motion surprised them both. He hadn't done this in a long time.

Too long, really.

"Mom, I'm fine. REALLY," he shifted uncomfortably in his chair, "besides, why don't you worry more about Rien? He's the one gone before the cock crows. All this time cooped up in an old, dusty Lycaenum with Father whatitsname…"

"Father Astor is teaching your brother wonderful skills… how to read and write… a literary education. It's very kind of him."

"Yes," Murain stifled the notion to roll his eyes, "but have you ever asked yourself why?"

She froze, emotion rose in her face but she said nothing.

"Mom… I…" She began to rise from her seat and walk away from the table. "Mom, it's just odd. Come on. Why Rien? It's all I'm asking…" Murain moodily starred at his half-finished bowl. Annoyance prickled his skin like mosquitoes.

"Your uniform and boots are pressed and cleaned next to the fire… dear," she said a bit stiffly as she wiped a stray lock of dark hair out of her face and tucked it behind her ear. The same color of hair testily swiped the clothes and boots and curtly walked out the door.

With a small sigh, she straightened her dress and patiently began cleaning up breakfast. Her hands lingered over the top of the chair at the head of the table. Worry still crinkled her forehead. Inside, something foreboded against today of all days. It was the same feeling a little over sixteen years ago when her husband had left to deliver a message to Shione. With a feeble, gentle little bit of hope, she forced herself to keep moving about the house, until the feelings dulled once again. Finally more or less satisfied, she dressed for the festival and went out into the village.

The morning of the festival all around her celebrated life and beauty laced with a coming excitement. The gates at the far end of the street were thrown wide. Already, strange visitors, fellow revelers from deeper on into Great Wood and storytellers or Waevers from all over the countryside were arriving alone, or in pairs or little groups of three or maybe five. Bright traveling cloaks in merry reds or greens, whites or sables, misty blues or deep browns filled the street. Tinkers and toymakers carted in their loads and began setting up little stands and stalls everywhere. Carrying her basket tightly, she made her way over the where the blacksmith was, just at the edge of a corner next to the town square outside where the towering stone Lycaenum stood. There, a humble little stall stood waiting for her. Kaylyn, the apprentice blacksmith girl, always set it up for her each year, ever since she was old enough to pick up the boards.

Kassandre smiled as she began setting out her cuts of venison Rien had been gathering. Some were fresh; others had been specially prepared with spices as jerky.

Townsfolk were beginning to pass by, most giving her warm, friendly nods. Everyone anticipated her stand. Reaching down into a side pocket of her basket, she carefully produced a neatly folded banner she and her two sons had made together several years ago. Proudly emblazoned with hand stitching, her sign read, "Sucat's Sweet Meats". Rien had written it - made sure the spelling and characters were correct. The green and silver banner flapped happily in the gathering breeze overhead. The general chatter began to swell all around as gradually more and more excited people - Rillians, and men - began drifting towards the square. The hum of the day grew imperceptibly as crowds came and went.

Around late morning the bards began showing up. Kassandre recognized many of them and waved - or politely asked of their health and their travels. Many of them were light-hearted and jovial - others, (the younger, newer ones, she thought) were quieter and nervous. Most came with instruments strapped on their backs or under their cloaks. But something new, she just began to notice, was how many of them came armed now. Sudden movements could spook them. Not a few cast dubious glances to the shadowy doorways or avoided the gazes of strangers.

"It is odd how in a community this small, there can be such large room for fear and doubt," commented Father Astor, suddenly appearing at Kassandre Sucat's side like a phantom, "It makes me wonder how safe we really are here..."

Kassandre only nodded, steeling her eyes against the sun, now reaching over the rooftops into her eyes. "Still not a bad crowd this year, by the looks of it, though..." she finally replied thoughtfully.

"True, and we have several new faces this year, it would seem," he said as a group of bards passed by, intently swapping strange tales.

No sooner had Astor finished speaking then a surly group of tall Rillians ambled past, each bearing a red tree painted on their tunics puffed out as brazenly defiant statements. Kassandre turned to Astor, whose steady gaze followed the dozen or so men as they steadily made their way towards the far end of the already milling village square. Catching a glimpse at some of their faces, something about them made her shiver... something about their vacant eyes. It was as if their iris' sparks never reached the surface.

She leaned her head back against the wooden support pillar next to her and sighed nervously. "More armed men." She muttered.

"Crusaders, by the looks of them, I would hazard."

"Crusaders?"

"Aye, Mrs. Sucat. They seek the fabled Red Tree far to the south. It's said it grants eternal life to all who eat of its fruit."

"Really," she said, nonplussed.

"So they say."

"So if young Rillian boys want to go pick distant apple trees, why do they need axes and swords for then?" She continued, fussing with her meats.

"Elves," replied Astor, quietly, as another group of crusaders passed nearby.

They both waited until the last Rillian passed, laughing loudly in response to some simple joke.

"Elves?"

"You might know them better as 'Woodspirits'. The elves claim the trees are sacred. They are holy things given to them by their wood god."

For a time they said nothing, content to watch the flood of festival-goers swirl by in bright colors.

The festival's mounting excitement seemed to seep into the blood. Children danced to little impromptu ditties played by indulgent troubadours. Stands filled up all around them with vendors, along with all manner of drinks and games and twinkling stars gradually unveiling all around them just like the first real stars of a summer's eve. A dozen different conversations echoed against the wood and stone walls of Nyrgen as the sun swiftly rose to its zenith. One of the questions on everybody's mind kept repeating in snatches every so often:

"Do you think she's coming?"

"Who?" the new or the very young might ask.

"Why, Veronjas, of course!"

"What's a Veronjas? Some kind of flower?"

"No silly, Veronjas is the Champion Waever! Weaves words into stories better than your mama weaves reeds into baskets. She's a Centaur, you know."

"OOOH... What's a Centau...?"

Then there she was, proudly emerging from underneath the far arching gate. Her long dark hair and large, luminous eyes sparkled in the dazzling high noon. She wore a smooth jerkin baring her long, smooth arms. Her long horse back and flanks were covered by a thick sort of mesh, the making to which was the envy of the village women and one of the many secrets of the somber Centauress. As she began to make her way steadily down Nyrgen's main street, an audible hush came over the nearby revelers. Reverent, almost. A cool, deep sort of peace seemed to emanate from her rich, dark brown eyes and quiet demeanor. Only the raucous laughter of the crusaders could be heard a lane or two over.

Veronjas made her way steadily nearer towards the square. Almost it seemed as if she would pass Kassandre by... but quicker than thought, she came to an abrupt halt.

Without turning, she finally spoke - her rich, vibrato voice a little deeper, yet with a still somehow sunny sort of timbre, "Astor," she smiled wide, flashing a brilliantly white smile.

"Veronjas, how are you my friend?" intoned the old Rillian looking only slightly down at her.

"I am well. The sun shines on our meeting, and ours, Lady Kassandre Sucat of Nyrgen," she said, bowing slightly and turning to face the corner booth.

Kassandre Sucat could never recall ever actually being this close to the decade and a half story-Waever champion. Swiftly composing herself, she stood and curtsied back and then caught herself laughing a little, "Waever Veronjas, hello..." she fumbled to voice her initial reactions, "It's just, I'm sorry... I've never been addressed 'Lady' before... it's for nobles... the mothers and daughters of queens..."

"And princes and kings," Veronjas finished.

Father Astor, looking past the Centauress at another trio of Rillians clad in dark emerald steadily drawing nearer. He smiled tightly and asked, "Veronjas, please, come refresh yourself in the Lycaenum, won't you?" Astor politely nodded towards Kassandre as he led the Centauress away, drawing her swiftly back into the milling crowds.

Kassandre watched as the tall men in long, sweeping emerald capes went flowing past. Their conical helms and nose-guards obscuring most of their faces. On their dark, padded leather cuirasses the sign of the royal trident broach flashed dangerously. As inquisitive gazes swept past she felt the irresistible urge to drop her face. Her long dark hair fell like a draped curtain between them. Pausing only long enough to pound a wanted poster roughly into a nearby pillar, they sauntered off. After a moment or two, they too were gone, lost amid the crowds.

After a reasonable pause, Kassandre took a moment to study the wanted poster. She had never learned to read, but the figure sketched on the parchment looked commanding and tough. She would have probably avoided ruffians like him anyway. Walking back to her booth, she resumed her cries, "Meat Pies! Jerky! Fresh Venison on a stick!" she announced after a moment's hesitation - just another voice calling out amid the masses on a festival day.

...

"Quickly, come inside," ushered Father Astor, opening a side door into the Lycaenum which had seemingly appeared from nowhere. Tucking an iron key with curious, looping wards away into the long crisp folds of his best brown tunic, he led his new guest swiftly out of the prying eyes of the eddying crowds. The cool air often accompanied with underground stone passages kissed the Centauress' skin as she entered the Lycaenum. Her eyes flicked up to a rune, fading fast, above the door's threshold and smiled knowingly.

"I do not recall ever using this entrance before, Astor," she said as they suddenly came out into a wide stone room.

"That was very foolish, Veronjas. I would have thought a Centauress would have known better."

Astor scolded, worry straining his voice. With a careless motion, he muttered a word and waved his hand. Candles and sconces suddenly flickered to life. "And the reason you have not used this door is, of course, because I was not here to open it for you. Runes like these are only visible to the ones who can make them, such as me. You'll only see them if I am nearby. Tricky things, I assure you." He said, bustling about the stone chamber. "If you were to get in your ridiculous equine head to try and force the door, it would probably be one of the last things you ever did."

"The stars foretold this day. Didn't you read the signs last night?" Replied the champion story Waever mistily.

"Don't pretend to hide behind your misty stargazer pretense. The boy's life is at stake..." Astor paced away, "now," he paused, "possibly the mother, too."

"But you knew this day would come. It will HAPPEN. It must happen. It is supposed to..."

"Just because they're stories doesn't make anything less real to the people in them!" snapped Father Astor, a fleeting shine of pleading glistened in the compassionate face," he blinked, "what signs?"

CRACK! ... Thump. A body fell over heavily just outside the door. The noise had come from where they had been, outside the Lycaenum, only a moment ago. Apparently, Astor's defensive runes were working.

"They are here. Assassins. And they will wait as long as is necessary… the wanted posters, what else Father?"

Astor whirled, clearly annoyed. "Yes. But I'm sure it was supposed to happen as well. What wanted posters??"

When Veronjas didn't say anything more, Astor huffed in disgust. "At least it's good to know I still have it, though…" he muttered.

For a moment there was silence and then…

…crack… a muffled cry of pain came from a high, piercing voice followed.

The pair paused.

After straining to listen for more, Veronjas spoke again, "Two down?"

Astor smirked and raised an eyebrow, "I thought you would already know…Ah, my friend, if only we were so lucky. The last cracking noise was far too quiet. No, I would say the unlucky recipient sustained only minor wounds. The last will be busy covering his fellow Queen's Man who is now dead, slumped outside a blank brick wall." His mind raced, the old feel of the game, always three steps ahead of the rest, began churning inside him again.

The Centauress took a short breath and tapped her fingers on her flank as if counting beats. Suddenly, she stopped. The air grew thick where they stood. As if the very fibers of their world could be felt, grain by grain. "Your Rillian Lord has a funny way of showing his authority… allowing his sister to all but rule his kingdom for him…"

Father Astor scowled but held his tongue.

After neither had spoken for a space, Veronjas took a breath and blinked, as if sensing some invisible change in the airs. "It is time now," was all she said.

…

Rien had taken off early with Soph, eagerly showing him around his humble village. As they went, Soph would relate his travels, and carefully listening to everything the Rillian explained about his life in Nyrgen. Turning up the main road, they saw the first early risers giving way to the growing festival crowds. Rien greeted acquaintances as they passed by. The mist in the village began clearing as the first rays of sun began filtering through. Everywhere the golden stars glinted light off their dewy frames. As the sun rose straight down the street, the flowers and the banners seemed to glow brighter. Coming near the square, they spotted Kaylyn coming out of the blacksmith. Behind her, the glowing forge simmered like dragon's fire, hazy in the lifting fog.

"Rien! Morning," she gasped, carrying heavy looking boards, "who's your little friend?" she asked, looking down on Soph.

"Oh, this is Soph – he's from The Isles of the Sea Kings!" Rien proudly explained.

"OOOH! Is that why you're so small, then?" she asked, smiling pleasantly.

For a moment, Rien was worried Soph might have been offended. But his tension whisked away as he watched the traveler stare back up at Kaylyn for a moment and then laugh and wave her question away… and then, quick as a wink, began scribbling away once more in his worn journal.

"Kaylyn - here, let me help you," Rien said, coming over to help, "setting up Mom's stand again?"

"No, I just like getting up early so I can carry heavy objects, why?" she scowled. But once they moved the wood over, she stretched and laughed, still half-eyeing Soph with curiosity. A loud yawn followed.

Soph walked over and looked at the lumber. Most of it was bigger than he was. Together, Rien and Kaylyn quickly assembled a sturdy booth. Soph replaced his journal after a final flourish and tried to help, but the traveler soon found he could only really lift the smallest of the Rillian-sized pieces.

Once they finished, Soph introduced himself as one of the competing storytellers (Waevers - Rien quickly reminded him).

"Oh, ok... I... you're going to laugh... I was wondering if you might be a Dwarf or something... is all," Kaylyn smiled.

"Oh, it's not a problem – I'm sure giants don't see humans too often here..."

Both Rien and Kaylyn stopped, confused. "Giants? What are those?"

Soph started flustering, "Oh, um... I, Rillians... Rillians. Sorry. New language and all," he muttered apologetically. "Must make a note..." he finished, whipping out his journal again, jotting hasty annotations.

Rien caught himself gazing at Kaylyn... her rosy cheeks flush from the forges fire and the physical exertion. Unnoticing, she pushed a stray lock behind her ear and yawned again.

From somewhere high above, a beautiful morning song burst into bloom. As if all the world's birds had synchronized into an otherworldly chorus. The few people out this time of morning paused where they were and what they were doing to listen. As the morning sun finally topped the rise of distant slanted roofs, all the colors seemed to glow vivid, and then the Firebird settled on Rien's shoulder.

"Show off," muttered Rien.

Soph gasped, marveling at the tongues living flames licking off the bird. The bird swiveled its head and gave the traveler a piercing sort of look, then began preening itself confidently.

"What IS this?? I noticed it the other night, but I didn't really know what to say or how to ask..." Soph asked, daring to take another step closer.

"It's trouble, is what it is," Rien said, gazing thoughtfully at the blazing bird, "Honestly, I don't really know... I found it in the woods a while ago and it's followed me around ever since. Father Astor called him a 'Firebird' or something... whatever it means..." The boy began stroking the bird absentmindedly.

Soph's face slowly transformed with some unspoken realization. Then he nearly fainted. "DO YOU KNOW WHAT THIS IS?!"

"No, what?" Kaylyn asked.

Soph made an odd sort of strangling noise and then fished out an old coin and held it up. The reverse image on the coin was a perfect imitation of the Firebird. "There is always, only, one," he repeated by heart as if reciting.

"Always one... what?" Rien asked.

Soph sighed. Around them now, the first early-comers of the festival began trickling in through the newly opened gates. The sizzling smells of village life crackled up everywhere now: families breaking their fasts, chatter, and dogs barking happily in the distance. A few passersby stopped to watch the odd fiery bird before ambling on. One man, in particular, stumbled by, stopped to stare Rien's way before stumbling on, muttering to himself.

"Do you know the first thing I did once I got to the Isle of the Wise and my college?" Soph asked.

Kaylyn raised her eyebrows.

"Hum. Let's see... I LOOKED UP EVERYTHING I POSSIBLY COULD OF THIS." He pointed to the coin, before whisking it back into his cloak. I wanted to know... as much as possible about vanishing men and strange coins. Everything, or better, if I could manage it. Do you even realize what this bird means? I..., of course, you don't..." He looked nervously around, acting suddenly suspicious of the obviously innocent early festival-goers. "Is there somewhere more private we can talk?" he eyed the looming Lycaenum across the square.

"Look, Rien. I have to get back with stuff for the festival and all - if Soph - your name, right?" Kaylyn double-checked, "If Soph here isn't too crazy, tell me about it later after the... dance... tonight..." she said, immediately regretting her poor wording.

Rien felt the air go out of his chest. He had almost forgotten all about it. "Yeah... sure. Come on Soph, we'll go head over to the Lycaenum... tell me more there..."

The pair trotted off, Rien tried his best to put a brave face on the bitter stab in his heart, and ignore his own swirling colors emanating out of him which the Firebird enabled him to see. Behind them, the girl lingered for a moment uncomfortably before pushing another long strand back behind an ear and doggedly continuing her morning chores.

With the Firebird riding contentedly on Rien's shoulder, the pair crossed the threshold of the main entrance to the Lycaenum. The smell of books filled their noses. Their skin felt the cool feel the tile and marble left in the air as the masonry lead them off into endless pathways of books. The records of all the greatest stories gathered from festival days long gone by stood stalwartly by at attention.

Soph appeared to be attempting to gasp and drool at once. A stray ember from the Firebird spiraled gracefully down chanced to touch his arm. Soph jumped, startled. While the speck was clearly on fire, he felt no pain.

"Yeah, it threw me off too, at first," Rien offered casually.

But Soph finally managed to regain his bursting at the seams composure, "Rien, I don't think you know what you have... did... um... I can't believe I'M the one asking you this, but I suppose it has to be someone..."

Rien looked down expectantly at Soph.

"Rien... did, did the Firebird choose you... at all... um... by chance?"

"Choose me? How do you mean? I found him in the woods like I said..." Rien offered vaguely, rubbing his chest absentmindedly.

But Soph saw right past Rien's bluff. "You have... the brand, don't you?" There was no lingering question left in his voice now.

"Brand... I... what do you mean?" He looked around sheepishly and then unlaced his shirt a little, revealing part of the Phoenix brand on his chest. "This?"

Soph stumbled. "Yes." He finally managed to squeak. After recovering again, he carefully looked up at Rien, furrowing his brows, "Odd how the bird would choose a Gia... I mean Rillian, though."

"I don't understand what you mean..." Rien said as he re-laced up his cotton festival shirt.

"There is always, only, ever, one Firebird, Rien. Not only are they exceedingly rare, they, or rather it, is the living symbol of the Elvish people. Life, art, rebirth, journey, the way, the path, the truth.

You... uh... haven't seen any red flowers around, by chance... shaped like miniature kings crowns...?" Soph hazarded.

Rien shivered involuntarily. The light of the beautiful girl flashed like sudden lightning, stirring his memory. "The one with little bells on the tips..." he said mechanically.

Soph's eyes, if possible, popped open even wider. "Where did you...? How did you...? Never mind. Never mind. Rien, I wonder if it might not be safe for you here. Have you ever heard of Firehall?"

"Nope," the boy shook his head.

"Far to the north, there is a place where the Great Forest touches the mountains. There under the fading leaves, lies the Elven capital for this land. There, it is written, is a fire which never goes out, lit to guide lost travelers to safety and warmth. It is said the trees themselves guard its borders, deterring the unworthy or enemies. From there, even the seasons themselves are ruled."

Rien felt far away. In his fertile mind's eye, he imagined the flickering fire and the whispering trees... and beside them stood the beautiful girl. For a spell, he forgot all about Kaylyn and even Leunami.

"Rien. Rien," Soph shook his arm.

Dazed, Rien slowly looked down. His ears gradually filled again with the rising sounds of the festival beginning just outside the thick oak doors.

Soph shook his head again. "Like I said, I can't believe I'M the one to tell you this... You ARE the Phoenix. I don't... I don't really know how to explain it... what with the circles being, ah, um... turned off? for all intents and purposes. It happened after the Fall, you know."

The boy tried to quickly cover the blank look which naturally filled his face until a timely nudge from Kadierie jostled his memory... "I... the bird showed me... I think. It was terrible." He shuddered again. "Look, I don't know about any of this... I was just off in the woods when it came along. I'm just a kid... I'm nothing special. I mean... I wish I was... but who doesn't? Right?"

Soph's face softened a bit, "there is no such thing as ordinary. Remember this."

After a space, Rien drew his gaze away from intently studying the funny rune carvings above the door, "Why Firehall?"

"Why Firehall. *Why Firehall?* Why Firehall! Rien, don't you know anythi..." But Soph stopped himself, seeing the hurt in Rien's face, "Look, I'm sorry. I forget you wouldn't be allowed to know much about barbarous Woodspirits. Not many do, to be completely honest. Rien, there isn't much time - there hasn't been since the Fall. Look, once upon a time, there were seven great circles which connected the whole land together. People, elves especially, would travel these ways... covering vast distances in the blink of an eye, in the space of a breath. But before the Fall, it is said Death had not yet come to this place," Soph paused to breathe for a moment.

Now it was Rien's turn for his eyes to bulge.

"There was plenty and life was good. The Circles just meant everybody could see each other whenever they liked, I think. Imagine being able to go see Lymwall - your capital - or even Old Rillium itself... whenever you wanted. You could live at the banks of Hesphoria, the great gulf far to the East, and pop in for lunch with your mom here in Nyrgen on a whim whenever you pleased. Imagine if loneliness was extinct. The old stories say incredible things about these circles - how they were made at the beginning. How they were guarded by dragons and griffins..." He took a breath and paced, hungrily eyeing the rows of books stretched away out in the next room and then shook his head and continued.

"The only trick was, you had to have a piece from one of the Great Circles in order to travel there. It's just another reason why elves like growing things you see... one can only take so many rocks, you know... but take a seed or better yet, water or even a book written in one... look, the point is one day, all the elves decided to gather a piece from each Circle together at their once great city far away to the south. On High Summer long ago, they gathered there for a grand ceremony. They wanted to put all the pieces together, to form the Eighth Circle."

"Why?"

"Excellent question, Rien," Soph eyed the books again. "Have you ever heard something you knew was true? It was something which you felt in your soul. Or a tale you were lost in? Someone suddenly interrupted you and you blinked, and suddenly you became aware again of the room and the chair you were sitting in the whole time? Have you ever daydreamed and forgotten where you were? Or watched a flame mesmerize you? There are other places. Other Realms! We dream about them all the time. We write about them. We imagine them. We think and talk about them. Your little festival today is actually a celebration of this great fact. Whenever you pick up a storybook, and you yearn to be there, in the world of its pages... this is it... this, as best as I can understand, is sort of what traveling by circles was like... a calling... yet unlike how our yearnings leave us still sitting in the room or staring out the window - through the Circles, you could actually go there."

"You mean there are other worlds? And you can go there just by reading a book?" Rien asked a little incredulously.

"So they say. It is why I traveled here to Dardania - this continent where you live. Where I live, we get books from the Whalers, who in turn get them from elves (we think) who live far to the north, beyond your Sable Lord's realm. Rien, like I said, they are not written in any known language of this world."

"How do you know?" Rien asked, staring out a window at the pantomiming revelers. Across the square, two men in sweeping robes were busy hammering up wanted posters brusquely.

Soph came and stood beside him and with care and deliberation asked, "Do you see the man walking past in Lincoln green with the red feather in his cap and a long yew bow and bristling quiver slung over his shoulder?"

Rien nodded.

"Watch."

The boy gasped. The man had turned and gazed directly at him, winked roguishly, and then vanished into thin air. Nobody in the crowd seemed to notice anything, not even the wanted-poster men, who had moved on down a cobblestone side street.

Rien turned towards Soph and took a few steps back. "H...h...how? How did you do...?"

Soph looked Rien square in the eyes, "because I said so. I said something out of a whaler's book, after a fashion. The language... it is... different... yet somehow the same. What I wouldn't give for a good dictionary or a book on syntax and grammar, though," he sighed and stared dreamily up at the rafters.

"What language? What did you say? I didn't hear anything different."

Soph rolled his eyes, "of course you heard me. But you are right in saying you didn't hear anything different."

Rien looked puzzled.

"I just asked you if you saw the man in Lincoln green with the red feather in his cap walking past.

As for why exactly you didn't hear a difference, I'm actually not quite sure yet," he explained, scratching his head.

Outside, Veronjas and Father Astor walked hurriedly through the crowd, bent on some mission or another. And then it hit him... "THAT's WHY SHE ALWAYS WINS."

"Why WHO wins, Rien?" Soph had his hand on the knob, about to enter the Lycaenum proper.

"Veronjas," he chuckled...

"The storyteller friend of yours? How?" Soph asked curiously, as he turned back to stand next to Rien, watching the Centauress tactfully negotiate the swelling crowd.

"I don't know. It was just a thought. It popped into my head just now. Look, test it."

Soph raised an eyebrow.

"Tonight at the storytelling contest - tell your story in this fancy other language of yours. If you can beat her, I'm wrong... but..."

Soph gazed steadily at his shifting feet, quietly.

"Hey! You were already planning on doing just this, weren't you?!" he laughed, "you cheater!"

"So... yes, about that, Rien... where do I sign up to compete, exactly?"

Outside, the Centauress and Astor could still be seen, weeding their way through the crowds, hunting intently for someone...

...

The long rays of day finally began to slink away past the jutting crooks and angles of the village. Blazing away at the edge of the world was the sun, slipping seamlessly into the cool breath of night. As dusk deepened, fireflies began shimmering, and the fires were lit with their arrival. In Nyrgen, the little village in the middle of the vastness of the Great Forest, the stars shone down, mingling with the festival stars already twinkling within. Ready, expectant and waiting. There, the humble little square was cleared. A calm night wind ruffled the banners and stirred the embers of the fires. In the flickering shadows, the long-awaited barding contest finally all began.

On a little stage just high enough to raise most speakers above the heads of their hushed audience, bard after bard told their tales. Far away and high above the night wore on as the varied voices bespoke their tales with the rise and the fall of the flames and the breathing of the breeze stirring the forest all around them. Sparks drifted determinedly up towards the heavens, where the rising moon accepted them like miniature libations. Enthralled, the revelers listened to story after story, unaware of the two prominent people so painfully missing from the night's ceremony.

Father Astor and Veronjas had spent the whole day searching intently for Rien. Somehow, at each turn, they had missed him. They had, however, stopped to read the new roughly painted wanted posters.

As Father Astor shook his head, his sagely beard waggled a bit, "oh Fy'el, my friend, what have you gotten yourself into this time...?"

When the Stories had been going on for a great while, they began to worry about how perhaps the dangerous Queen's Men had already snatched the boy. Thankfully, they noticed one of the remaining agents lingering near a particularly bright iron sconce, favoring a pronouncedly bad limp.

"Great. Rien is now nowhere to be found. But I suppose you saw this coming as well, my four-legged friend," grumbled Astor, removing his spectacles to clean them worriedly.

Veronjas shot him a deep, silent look. "I must give my Story soon; otherwise they will know something is amiss tonight." She looked up at the stars. So many benign blinking lights filled the skies, so many signs, so many purposes. And she did her best to keep track of them all. "Yes, now is the time to go..." she stopped. Up near the Waever's stage, was a man, dwarfed among the Rillian crowd. She took him for a man, perhaps from the islands of the deep. But his voice... his words as he began... they swelled up. They enraptured the entranced crowd.

"Astor," she hissed.

"Hmm... what? Not now, this young man is speaking..." he murmured.

She shook him gently, "Astor, he is speaking my words! Mine!"

Father Astor shook his head, attempting to snap out it. "Veronjas, this is very un-Centaurish of you. What do you mean? Your words? Are you sure this isn't merely jealousy talking, instead?"

"The time for me to explain is later - look!" she said, struggling to keep her indignant voice down.

Following her slender, pointing arm, Astor saw perched on an eave near the stage, was the Firebird. Quickly, he glanced back to the Queen's Man, still leaning mesmerized against the pole, intently watching the new speaker along with the rest of the enchanted audience. "Now is our chance. Rien can't be far from the Firebird."

They gently parted the crowd, both desperately praying they could reach the boy in time. There. The shifting bodies momentarily swayed just enough for Astor, who was slightly taller than Veronjas, to catch a glimpse of the enraptured boy standing just underneath the roof where they had seen the Firebird earlier. Briefly, the shuffling crowd separated Astor from the Centauress. They determinedly continued making their way, hoping the long-winded new storyteller would continue just a bit longer.

"I'll give him first prize... I promise... just keep talking," Astor worried, glancing back at the still mercifully oblivious agent.

Only a few more yards remained now. Astor turned the corner and just managed to squeeze past a group of particularly well-fed Rillians... And then... the boardwalk where Rien had only moments ago loitered was now empty. Ice filled the old man's veins.

"Oh Poseidon, protect him! Help me to find him," he silently prayed. His heart pounded away as he quickly glanced around. Without thinking, Father Astor quickly took a right and rounded the corner of the Lycaenum. The shadows were thickest here, away from the light and all the still-listening people. Noiselessly, he padded down the alley. Up ahead Astor thought he could make out voices…

…

Rien gasped. Before him loomed a tall Rillian with a cunning grin and a long jagged knife. All around them the air was still… as if some fastness had closed in around them… The man had long since dropped his overly enthusiastic smile and friendly manner.

"Where's my mother?" Rien demanded while attempting to back slowly away from the very sharp knife.

Only stony silence greeted him from the cold man.

Rien glanced around. "You said she needed me. Where is she? You said she would be here. If…" horror flooded his mind, steeling his growing panic, "If you've done something to her, I'll… I'll…"

The man just raised his dark eyebrows and donned a mocking expression. Somewhere floating in the northward breeze, Rien could just make out Soph beginning to wind down his tale. The knife-wielding man licked his lips, counting the seconds before; at long last, he would be vindicated from failure. Sixteen years of failure, to be precise. Oh, how she would reward him. An irrepressible shiver of trepidation and pleasure snaked down his spine. He idly eyed his poised knife… a shadow of a thought flickered through his already made-up mind… suppose he told him… told the little brat just a little bit… just a tincy bit. Why would it matter…? It might be fun…

"Your mother isn't here," his voice sliced through the silence. The sudden sound made the boy jump. He stumbled behind something hidden in the curtains of ivy adorning the wall of the Lycaenum. A body! There was just enough light to see an identical brooch on the body to one of the men here to kill Rien.

Rien's mind whirled. Trying to force himself to reason, he fought to string a few feeble facts together… they might be the last he ever had… The dead man… there must be friends out here tonight. The boy took another step back, bumping into the next building's wall. The silvery knife seemed to float through the air, following him.

The man spoke again, "You don't even know why I'm here. Shhh… Shh… It's ok. It's ok. I do. We missed you sixteen years ago. A pity. A mistake. If it wasn't for the Spymaster's meddling… well… all's well as ends well… it won't matter to you soon enough."

Rien's throat was as dry as death, but his voice rasped out, "what won't matter?"

The man's eyes never left the spot along the boy's throat where he intended to make the first cut. "Why, you of course. It was always about you. Clever really, hiding here in this dump of a village. More of a hovel, really. But let's not mince words, shall we?" He pointed to his brooch with his free hand. "See this? This means I'm a Queen's Man. An agent of Her Majesty, the Emerald Queen. A Queen who will last a thousand years! Or more. A Queen who will rule. And no upstart bastard heir will stand in her way," his eyes glinted with cruel amusement at the boy's answering confusion. "Ah yes. Yes. YESSS. He's beginning to put it together… Go ahead… I'll grant you a few more precious moments before I end you. Figure it out."

Rien's mind raced. He didn't understand what this madman was going on about… desperately, he groped behind him, sticking his trembling hands into the ivy for something – anything - he could use to defend himself with.

"*Prince* Rien? Disgusting!" the man spat, "ever wonder why your little majesty is shorter than all the other kids… a bit nimbler… a bit lither…? We've been watching you," the man's eyes adopted a dead sort of glint as if something behind them was chuckling uncontrollably at some psychotic joke, "You and your love for non-Rillians. Filth. Rillians are children of the gods. We will rule. We will take the Tree of Life and live forever. We will have dominion. Over everything. And the Queen will take us there. Her Majesty has seen it. And it will be so. All Hail the Queen!" as he cried fanatically, he lunged in one deadly motion.

Above Rien, a bright, shimmering blue rune of an 'A' appeared. Instinctively he leaped aside as burning sensation sliced at his chest. He stumbled away, scrambling on his hands and knees, gasping for air. Suddenly, he was enveloped by brown folds of robe. Long, bristly beard filled his vision and a warm, familiar scent embraced him. He started blindly punching. But strong arms held him still until he quit struggling and looked up.

Father Astor gazed back down at the boy he considered like a son. For all those years Astor had watched over the boy... the realization of how it must all be different now flooded the old man. It must all change. Father Astor pushed back the terrified boy's ruffled hair and knelt down so they were now at eye level. With a word, he waved his hand over Rien's bleeding side. Rien shook uncontrollably, glancing back at the crumpled heap of the Rillian who had just tried to murder him. Now, the once imposing man was only a deposited jumble of splayed limbs sticking out at odd angles next to the other dead agent.

Vaguely behind them, they could hear Soph finishing his long tale followed by thunderous applause. Suddenly, the dark alley filled with a blazing, fiery light as the Firebird dove down, incinerating the would-be assailant's forms with a fierce flame. The sudden illumination quickly died away under the long dark shadows of the tall Rillian buildings flanking the alleyway.

"I am so sorry, Rien. I had to stall him by suggesting he talk... it was the only way... his knife was so close to you..." the old man said. Astor felt as if he really had lived a thousand years now... so much weight clamped down on his chest. "So I used what I had. And thankfully I am familiar with the type of poison these people use... you are safe for now," his eyes flicked up to the still flickering blue rune, "but men like this one will keep coming for so long as they know you live. Listen, now Rien. You must go. Leave at once. Head north, for a place named Firehall. You will be safe there, of all places."

Rien felt his quivering lips move, "Firehall?" Is it true, what h... what he said?"

"Yes, my son. Firehall. It is the capital of the Elves of Greatwood away to the north, at the feet of the Norran Mountains. The Forest around it protects it and dissuades even the craftiest of prying eyes...but I think, in your case, the trees will let you in... you'll see. Go at once, as true north as you can now – I will speak with your mother, and alert the friends I have across the Great Forest to watch for you."

Rien, still in shock, forced his mouth to open with one last question, "Is it true, what h... what the Queen's Man said?"

Behind the silhouetted pair, the crowd began to mill again. A few curious on-lookers who had seen the fiery bird flare up had begun to drift disinterestedly away now. Apparently whatever fun there was to be had was now finished. In the distance, the queen's man who had only a moment ago been enthralled by the story whisked away into the night.

Father Astor looked into the eyes of the boy. An eternity seemed to flash by in a single breath.

He sighed.

"It is true, my son."

Chapter IV
Flight

Rien was exhausted. Every muscle he knew, and a few he didn't, were burning and quivering from the non-stop exertion. Singular thoughts floated through his deadened head like stray stars. He had fled that very night, at the urging of Father Astor. Guided by Soph's suggestion of the sanctuary Firehall might provide, Rien scrambled on and on. Forcefully, the boy chose not to even begin to try and imagine how his mother would react after Father Astor met with her... Desperately, he had wished Father Astor or Veronjas had come with him... Even though the old man had reassured Rien help would find him, the boy couldn't help but feel the subtle grip of icy terror behind every strange tree-shadow and woodland noise.

"Rest. Sleep. Must find the box," he thought – for Rien had not forgotten about his one last possession hidden away in the old ruins to the south of Nyrgen.

Panting, he gazed ahead at a large hill. Atop it, crumbling masonry stood, once white, now long faded into grey. The ghostly ruins seemed to shift in the impenetrable forest fog. The moss grew in thick, lush carpets amid the tall, pitted pillars Rien wearily stumbled past. Vibrant ferns stretched and bowed under the glow of gracious starlight as the drained youth brushed through them.

Overhead, a grand vaulted dome, half fallen through, still bespoke a majestic painting in deep royal blues and silvers. Luminous light trickled through, splashing onto the ground at Rien's boots. Leafy emerald vines spiraled crazily up into the quiet darkness of the forest canopy. High above, the twinkling sound of chimes sounded as water softly fell. All around, it seemed a deep, peaceful presence had long ago chosen this tumbled Elven ruin as home.

Through his heavy, drooping eyelids, Rien could sense the echoes of warm memories coursing through the aged stone walls surrounding him. And then up ahead came what he desperately desired most: flames' shadows flickering mysteriously upon smooth marble walls. Relief ignited on a near unconscious level through Rien's mind. He stepped through one final archway which was missing a capstone. With end in sight, Rien put one lead-like boot-step in front of the other tottering through a spacious, circular stone courtyard.

"The box is under the statue. Right where I hid…" muttered Rien as he finally succumbed to the irresistible arms of sleep at last.

The Firebird, who had been fluttering after the boy, cozied up gently next to his sleeping form. Its hypnotic flames warmed Rien's chilled skin, chasing away the cold forest air better than any bonfire could have. There amidst the ruins of the lost city, the boy slept on and the bird kept watch. Time passed. The trees which had grown up with time through the cracking mortar swayed with the breeze. Night enveloped the pair. The sounds and deft movements of the forest and its nocturnal inhabitants carried on their careless symphony, seemingly unaware of their new audience members.

Sometime past the zenith of the moon, a large figure crashed through a clearing at the outskirts of the ruins some distance away. Murain had been doing his best at tracking his brother's deft trail. Used to following giant footfalls, his brother's markedly smaller impressions had been difficult in the dark woods. But he had managed it. And here, before him loomed great white pillars and roofless buildings, cracked and crumbling in the starlight. The eerily beautiful ruins gave Murain the creeps. Rien's older brother knew as plain as day, by design, these were obviously no proper Rillian structures - otherwise, they would not have become forlorn wrecks, forgotten out in the middle of nowhere in the woods.

The growing feeling of danger had been bothering Murain all evening – but it hadn't been after the festival had concluded, without his younger brother's long-expected performance he had known something was amiss. Sure he had danced with Kaylyn –which went great as far as he could tell… but he had felt oddly distant the whole time. She had noticed it too, especially after he left immediately afterward. Something was wrong. He was sure of it.

Swiftly, Murain had searched the village for Rien. Once he had seen the horse-woman and that old Astor fellow scuttling about… but… nothing. Finally, by sheer luck, he had run into Addios who had mentioned seeing Rien slip by, hurrying down the street towards the gates, which had been left standing open for the crowds of festival goers.

"By the abuses of that guard S'ven… I knew instantly it had been Rien leaving. But your brother didn't even turn to antagonize him back like he usually does… He just sprinted off… I think he turned left before it gets shadowy out of the gate torchlight," Addios had wordily explained.

Murain wrenched his mind back onto the task at hand – eyeing the ruins dubiously. "Probably Woodspirit haunts…" he muttered, suppressing a shiver. His sweat had gone suddenly cold in the night air after he had ceased tracking. His eyes glanced around the broken masonry. The stones were hard to make out in the dark, yet they seemed to still glow with some unnatural light. Somewhere inside, the youth longed for solid Rillian walls and his familiar home… for his younger brother lazing there, sleeping late in the morning sun across their room they shared.

Stumbling out of a yawning archway, Murain suddenly found his quarry. A dark figure bathed in deep reds of flickering embers lay near a fire (or was it a bird?) in a deep sleep. Towering over the figure, a once impressive statue still stood, its face worn almost beyond all recognition. There he was: Rien.

Relief and anger simultaneously flooded Murain's veins. His brother's familiar form was just visible in the dull red light emanating from the strange bird Rien had so recently become inseparable from. Murain frowned. It wasn't Rillian. It wasn't right. This whole thing was so wrong. Rien just ran off? Besides not even competing and being formally entered into the Lycaenum – finally picking a Rillian profession… he just had run off… again. There was simple and then there was… odd - strange, even. Their mother would probably be furious at being shamed once again by his weird little brother…

The recent events from the festival flickered in the tall Rillian's mind with the dance of the flickering embers. The dancing lights lit up Murain's huge form against the jagged pillars and crumbling masonry behind him. His shadow jumped and crouched as it flitted among the ruined city.

Approaching, he saw in his brother's hands, a strange wooden box - an emblem emblazoned with the fiery bird which now eyed him warily from atop a faceless statue from which it had just now fluttered to.

He shivered. The whole place felt eerie: as if everything was listening to him. Murain decided he didn't like it as he gazed back down at the slumbering form of his brother. Rien's defected-looking pointed ears poking up from his sandy hair. The idea floated vaguely through Murain's mind to wake Rien and drag him back through the woods to their home that very tonight...

Idly, the older brother scratched his shirt. It was new: compliments of Murain's new friends. The Crusaders. The stories they told... now those were something Murain could get on board with. Living forever. Forever. The idea strained the brother's imagination. Incredible. And somewhere, deep in his heart, Murain felt the rumbling growl of lust. He wanted more... more everything. It was like an ache. A cancer. He could feel the slow, inevitable decay of time dripping away like lifeblood from his veins. Murain gazed up at the night sky, searching for the constellations he knew well after nights of tracking in the dark for the militia. Blues and greens - reds and pearly white stars blinked and gazed back down at him. He remained serene and unaware of the growing anger in his chest. Murain could never have quite said when it precisely had begun... but when he looked down at his brother... something bothered him. Something wasn't quite right. And Murain was sick and tired of his brother not acting properly.

Somewhere not far off, an owl hooted loudly. The sound, though fairly soft and indistinct, shattered the forest silence like breaking glass.

Rien stirred. Half cracking an eye, he jumped when his blue-green eyes came into focus. A giant of a Rillian was looming over him. It was enough to make anyone back away quickly, but Rien wasn't just anyone. He was Murain's brother. For a moment, neither spoke. Rien could just make out the flash of his brother's eyes. The icy silence exuding from his brother made him shiver, despite the Firebird's pervasive warmth. The younger brother's eyes flicked down to the odd symbol emblazoned on what was obviously a new shirt, which ruffled in the night breeze. Rien opened his mouth to say something and then shut it again. For the first time in his life, he felt strangely aware he was actually afraid of his own brother.

"You missed a lot after you left," Murain finally remarked.

Those same words would have meant much less to brothers who had never known their father.

High above, the heavens veiled as thick clouds rolled across the stars and waning moon. The only light now came from the Phoenix, and a weird straining glint from Murain's eyes flashing dangerously in the dark.

"They chased your four-legged wood demon out... the one you like so much... the horse-woman. 'Rillians deserve better,' they said..." Murain continued, bearing down on his brother, "I for one agree. It's what killed old Voros... I bet you didn't know... horse-things killed him and left him for dead. We can't trust murderers. And Woodspirits?" he said eyeing the surrounding ruins with obvious disgust. They're the ones..." the older brother began to pace, just at the edge of the firelight.

Rien slowly rose. The whole thing felt like a bad dream. The wind in the trees sighed and moaned... and somehow, deep in his heart lurked the fresh terror, once again. What he had seen not too many nights before - the battle - the killing... the dead and worse... his brother kept ranting words Rien knew weren't really his own. The younger brother swallowed and tried to steel himself. Standing straight and taking a breath, he waited until Murain's tirade paused.

"Murain. I have to go," Rien blurted, interrupting Murain's rant.

His older brother's eyes narrowed into horizontal slits. A vein in his temple popped.

Rien thought Murain would yell or lunge - start swinging or something - anything. But instead, freezing silence filled the space between them. "I... I don't know if I can quite explain it myself, but I have to go..." He looked up at his brother... hoping maybe there would be some sort of understanding somewhere... but only a glare answered him. Rien started gathering his things... ensuring he had his precious box, stuffing his pack and slinging his bow he slowly, achingly began trudging off in a vaguely northerly direction, towards the elusive Firehall of the Woodspirits.

Behind him, his brother's angered voice sliced through the air, "Leaving... Just like dad did."

Rien stopped. All the years of abandonment and anger welled up in him suddenly. Every time he had been singled out or picked on. Each awkward meal their mother had stared at the fourth chair around the table – eternally and accusingly empty.

"Shut up!" Rien suddenly shouted. If he hadn't of been furious he would have been crying. It was like some sort of torrential flood had been unplugged inside him somewhere. "Murain! Someone tried to KILL me back at the festival. With a knife. In an alley. Queen's Men, I think. The ones working WITH the crusaders. I... I think... I think the Queen wants me dead."

"The QUEEN? Why?"

"I... um... They think I'm a prince or something... They think I am the heir. I think we had a different father. It's why I have to go," with a willed effort, he tried to suppress some of his welling anger, "Just try... try and understand."

Murain, momentarily shocked, whipped around to face his younger brother. His cold eyes piercing his brother like daggers. "You're just like Dad. You think you're so great and special. You make friends with non-Rillians and abandon your own family. You walk out on Mom. You leave me. COWARD! You deserve..."

"What? Death?!" Rien shouted back. "Did your Crusader friends tell you to say that too?! Can't you see how twisted you are? You've been playing the hero all these years... trying so hard with the militia and all the girls. Everything about you is perfect except you. The real you. I know. I'm your brother. If anything, you're the one running away. Only, you already have the perfect pretext... oh, look at me... I'm Murain - I'm a CRUSADER now... look at me... I..."

Murain jumped at Rien, fists flying. The pair tumbled, kicking and pummeling. Cuts and bruises began blossoming all over the two brothers. Suddenly, with a blinding, fiery flash, the Firebird soared down in between them. A wall of flames erupted, separating them. The fire lasted for only a moment, but if Rien hadn't have been so furious, he would have noticed the split-second form silhouetted in the inferno's center. Blasted backward, both boys lay momentarily sprawled wherever they had fallen. Rien had been lucky. Picking himself up from a patch of rank weeds poking up between the cracked stones he saw Murain, some distance away, lying in a crumpled heap next to thick pillars, apparently unconscious. A faint trickle of blood glistened in the remnants of the sparking fire as it gradually settled back down into the form of the tense bird.

The Firebird swept back its wings with a fierce glare and settled territorially onto its customary spot on Rien's shoulder. Then, it cried a terrible cry as it took flight once more. The younger brother saw it more than heard it... but all the colors swirling around him and the distant form of his incapacitated older brother made him gasp.

Rien realized he had heard this cry before... in his dreams. The terrible visions of the Great City so full of life and light... now a smoldering ruin of death... Everything felt singular, as if then and now were somehow one. He blinked and saw all the jagged ruins, saw the faceless statue lit by fire... and it felt like all the fear, terror and chaos of the past and the present enveloped him.

He ran. High above, the Firebird flew, following Rien north amid the thickening forest darkness.

And out of the sylvan gloom rang a familiar hoarse voice, "Rien! Rien Sucat! You're no brother of mine!"

And on and on Rien ran and ran...

...

Rien's tale continues in _Rienspel Issue III: The Rangers_

Or

Purchase the complete first volume:
The Phoenix of Redd, Volume I: Rienspel

About the Author

Ryan P. Freeman is a fellow adventurer. After miraculously surviving childhood cancer, he launched into talk radio. Ryan is a pastor, former International Red Cross speaker, and medieval-enthusiast; loves sampling craft-beers, and is an unapologetically proud kilt-wearer. His interests range from exploring real-world pan-mythology to survivalist camping and copious video gaming. Ryan also writes for *The Scribe*, an online literary magazine based out of St Louis, is a proud member of the St Louis and Missouri Writers Guilds, and is the founder of the Hannibal Writers Guild.

Learn more about Ryan here: www.ryanpfreeman.com.

Made in the USA
Middletown, DE
02 April 2021

36839902R20031